WHIPPING THE CAT

Tales from Lough Neagh's banks

Patrick Smyth

Illustrations; John O'Neill

First published 1993 by
Patrick Smyth, Marymount, Lurgan, Co. Armagh.

© 1993 Patrick Smyth

ISBN 0 9518153 1 8

Text set in 10 pt. Times Roman

Layout and typesetting:-
Irish World
Irish World House
26 Market Square
Dungannon.

Printed by Banbridge Chronicle Press Ltd.

Booksellers' enquiries:
P. Smyth, Telephone Lurgan (0762) 323098

ACKNOWLEDGEMENTS

I am deeply indebted to many people for invaluable help in the production of this volume, and I wish to take this opportunity to express my appreciation. In particular I wish to thank the following:

My grandson John O'Neill for all the illustrations except that of "the poor man in need of a wee bit of help", which has been reproduced from one of my earlier books. It was drawn by Brendan Tallon of Derrymore. John O'Neill is a Dubliner and currently a student at U.C.D.

Willie O'Kane, Publications Officer with Irish World, Dungannon, and his staff, for help with the layout and preparation of the text for printing.

Mary McKavanagh - my near neighbour and an expert and dedicated typist - for unravelling the manuscript and producing an impeccable typescript.

Brendan, John and Christie Hannon of Moss Road, Aghagallon for allowing me to photograph their colourful flock of Rhode Island Reds for the cover picture.

Mrs McNulty, Editor with Friars Bush Press, and Dr Bill Crawford, Director of the Federation for Ulster Local Studies, for providing expert advice and friendly encouragement.

Finally, my wife, Ethna, and a select group of other willing helpers for acting as mentors and patiently undertaking the proof reading duties.

ABOUT THE AUTHOR

Pat Smyth has lived in Lurgan for the past 40 years. He grew up on a small farm at Ballykeel in south west Antrim and entered the Stormont Civil Service from Lurgan Technical College at the age of 19. He rose to the Administrative grade and retired early to practise as a marketing and P.R. consultant. Later he took up freelance journalism and has been a newspaper columnist for the past ten years.

'Whipping the Cat' is his fourth book. In 1987 he published *'Memories of Old Lurgan'*, in 1988 *'Fireside Gleanings'* and in 1991 *'Osier Culture and Basketmaking'*. The first two books, both now out of print, were written with local business sponsorship under the pen name 'Alfie Tallon', while the third was grant-aided by the Ulster Local History Trust. All three have been best-sellers locally and have received widespread favourable reviews. Overseas sales have also been significant.

Pat is now established as an authority on local history and folklore. His style is anecdotal and his ability to reproduce the authentic spoken word has attracted favourable comment from many literary critics.

FOREWORD

When Pat Smyth was working on his study of basket-making and osier culture on the shores of Lough Neagh, he had to be restrained from adding stories relating to his childhood in and around the lough shore. It was facinating to realise how this study was recalling for him so many incidents and personalities. It was intriguing to see how he could get inside the skin of other folk like Anthony Duck, Master Lynch and Miss Morrison, and enjoyed such characters as William Wilson in *A Man of Consequence,* and *Annabella.* Through them, we begin to realise the poverty of the countryside in the days before the Welfare State and the problems of raising children on the family farm. For youngsters there was plenty of work, recalled in detail in *Robbing the Wild Bees* and *Horse Sense,* and there were tradesmen to watch, as in *Whipping the Cat* and *Dick the Butcher.* These people were no fools, and they all had their strategies for survival in a world that was very different from ours.

Bill Crawford
Federation for Ulster Local Studies

CONTENTS

THE UGLY BROWN LINE

Master Lynch had a 'Don't want to see anyone,' expression as he hurried out of Aghakeel chapel with his boy Brendan. Gaggles of gossiping gawkers crowding the threshold irritated him and he barely acknowledged their greetings. They made way for him silently and sympathetically, conscious of the sadness of the occasion for him.

Molly Watson, Jenny Johnston, Maggie Campbell and Alice Loughran had also hurried out and they were already at their usual vantage point, just inside the gate, so as to give everyone coming out of church the once-over. As soon as Lynch emerged their tongues started rattling.

Maggie was first. "My goodness," she exclaimed," doesn't the Master look ill. He's away to scrapings, and I don't like his colour."

"Right enough," Alice said, "He's like death warmed up. He was vexed enough about this border business; now Brigid's death has knocked the heart clean out of him completely."

"Wouldn't you just love to take him and that lad of his home and set them down to a good meal," Maggie remarked.

"Heavens! You had better not let bossie Annie Lyttle hear you say that, Maggie,she'll eat the face off you," said Jenny. "Why the Master doesn't get someone better than her to keep house for him, beats me. Bossie Annie could hardly boil hot water. Mrs. Lynch hadn't a word to say when she was alive and I hear the Master and Brendan are no better off. They just have to take it or leave it with that oul bag.

"The Master is tough enough with Brendan. Our Joe says he slaps him nearly every day in school for not knowing his lessons. If he would stand up to that oul termagant of a housekeeper I would think more of him. I suppose he is determined to have Brendan ahead of everyone else when his time comes to go to College in Cork. There is no school here good enough for Lynch's children! Cork people are very clannish."

"The Master" had only one buddy in the whole parish although he had been schoolmaster for 20 years, - old Frank Carville ..... an uneducated country yokel, but a long-headed old boy whose droll remarks always gave Lynch a bit of a lift.

Frank always loitered inside the chapel door gasping for a smoke and as usual he was already out on the road waiting for "the Master."

"Ach! It's great to see you Frank. Come on down to the house. I need company. I dread going in without Brigid and the wee girl. Brendan has cried on and off all morning."

Frank fell in step with the two of them and Lynch relaxed a bit as Frank rehearsed some of the cracks he had heard while the Master had been down south - now and then pausing to make an anxious enquiry about how "my wee girl" - Lynch's teenage daughter Maureen, was settling in at the convent school in Cork.

Lynch had been very upset by political developments in what he termed "The Black North" even before his wife had taken ill. With the partition of the country and the setting up of a Unionist Government for the six counties, he felt trapped in an alien place. He had been convinced that the Dublin Castle administration and the bishops would never give the Unionist regime control of the Catholic schools. They had held out for a while and he had foolishly boasted that he would never go on the payroll of Craig's Ministry of Education. But Dublin, and the Catholic Hierarchy, had let him down, and he hadn't been able to hold his head up since. As "The Master," he had always been accorded leadership in the parish. Now that he was taking his pay from the Unionists, he felt that many in the community looked on him as a broken reed and a renegade.

As he passed the school a sudden dread hit him that he might have an Inspector on his doorstep next morning and he decided to go in at once and pick up some papers which he needed to finalise. When he stepped into the dingy empty classroom his assistant, Joan Kelly's, overall hanging on a peg reminded him that, according to local gossip, she was one of the ones who had sneered behind his back about his climb down. "Ah, to heck with 'aul gander neck," he muttered. (Joan was a lanky lady with bottle shoulders and a long neck, and all the youngsters called her 'aul gander neck.').

When he headed for home again, memories of his return to Aghakeel on the Sunday after his honeymoon hit him, in spite of Frank's chatter. He recalled how Brigid had caused a real sensation by parading to Mass in their wedding attire. She

4

had been a picture in her white frock and veil, and Aghakeel folk told him afterwards that they had never seen anything so nice. Brigid had had to explain to them that it was always done that way in Carrigtohill, where she came from. That had been sixteen years ago, he mused .... yet it seemed so short a time.

Next morning he was back on the treadmill in school. 'Aul gander neck' was screeching at her scholars, as usual, before she was right into the classroom and he felt like telling her to shut up, but he had to leave her alone. He had never felt so depressed and he sensed that the children were watching his every move (as indeed they were). This increased the growing sensation that he had that he was hemmed in, with no obvious way out.

The run-down schoolhouse with its dingy interior and dilapidated furniture was no worse than any other of its day, or very little, but Lynch noticed it more. He had been at the parish priest about having it re-decorated, but Father McKillop wouldn't spend a penny, and the master had to put up with the state of affairs. Now he began to speculate on the possibility of looking for a transfer. The realisation that a move south of the border would be virtually impossible now, with two different education authorities to deal with, increased his gowing feelings of frustration. For the first time in his experience, old walls and ill-clad, unwashed groups of scholars seemed to close in on him, although the classroom was no more overcrowded than it always had been.

There weren't enough seats in the classroom for all the pupils and he always had to teach one class while they stood in a semi-circle. He had a line chalked on the grimy floor and he was accustomed to shouting, "Get back to the line." ..... Sometimes he would have flung his heavy pointer at the shins of some boy who had been heedless. Since all were barefooted in summer this usually woke up the day dreamer. On this particular morning he put the fourth class to study the geography of Ireland. They had to stand facing a wall map with a chosen boy leading them as they recited the names of the provinces, counties, principal towns, rivers, etc., parrot-wise *ad infinitum*. They were at this when the parish priest's odd-job man, Dick Magee, arrived with a ladder and some other tools. He had a sign board under his arm and he came in to show this to Lynch. It was inscribed AGHAKEEL PUBLIC ELEMENTARY SCHOOL and he explained that he was to take down the NATIONAL SCHOOL one and put up the new one.

Lynch immediately flew into a rage. "You can take that thing and burn it, Dick, it's not going up here," he bellowed. Poor Dick was shattered, "But Father O'Hare sent me, Master. I have to do what he tells me!"

"Here, give it to me, Dick," Lynch growled, "I'll take responsibility."

Dick did as he was told and Lynch promptly dumped the new board on top of a high press, raising a shower of dust. Dick went out, picked up his ladder, and silently marched off to the parochial house nearby, very angry.

It wasn't long till he was back, with Father O'Hare in tow. An argument ensued, but eventually Lynch had to calm down when Father O'Hare warned him that the Ministry were adamant that the new board had to go up and there was always the possibility that grant-aid would be put at risk if they didn't comply.

Lynch was in a vile temper for the rest of the day and often the pointer was sent flying at some lad's shins, even before he had had a warning. Others received four-of-the-best (administered on the palm of the hand with the same pointer) for minor misdemeanours. Even 'aul gander neck," began to look quizzically at Lynch's display of bad temper, but she said nothing, which just as well for Lynch was in a truculent mood. He regarded the compulsory change of name for schools as another swipe at the nationalists, and PUBLIC ELEMENTARY as the thin edge of socialism.

When he got an opportunity, he paused to hear how the boys around the map were getting on and put a couple of test questions. As they rhymed off the 32 counties, the four provinces, etc., as if the border did not exist, he got impish satisfaction in listening to them. "Them and their English border," he muttered and he made up his mind that he would not let *them* change the geography of Ireland, one and undivided, as far as his pupils were concerned.

As time went on, a burning feeling of resentment rankled with him. He also had a growing guilt complex in relation to his wife's death. If he had not brought her to Aghakeel and its chill winds of the Lough Neagh basin, and the rotten damp living conditions of houses in the Montiaghs, she would still be alive, he kept telling himself.

His health continued to deteriorate and he got a phobia about the possibility of contracting T. B. himself. He was well aware that some of his scholars who had bad coughs came from families riddled by the disease. One boy, Willie Lavery, had died from it a few months earlier. The stark reality of the unhealthy conditions in the single apartment school house began to prey more and more on his mind, but when he broached the subject with Miss Kelly, she just laughed. Obviously they didn't worry her - but then she was a local woman.

There was no water laid on, inside or outside the school. Drinks had to be cadged for residents in nearby cottages by boys who asked to get out, for the pump owned by the district council never functioned without priming. Some residents were abrasive, others like Liza Anne Drayney, who were very kind, got the most trade in drinks. Her brother Hughie, a chubby little man who worked as a roadman was universally known as "Hughie Beetle." He wasn't popular at all. He certainly resembled the traditional tool used for making champ and was less tolerant of door-knockers than Liza.

Even the sweeping of the classroom floor worried him now. A sprinkling can had to be taken each afternoon to the priest's house behind the school to be filled with water. The boy who fetched it sprinkled the floor liberally, while two others followed through with brooms. Getting out to fetch the water was actually regarded as a treat - so much so that nice judgement was needed around 2.45 pm to get in first with the plea, "Please Sir, can I go for the water?" To ask prematurely was a mini-disaster. Lynch reacted quite sharply. As the 'lucky' boys wielded short-handled brooms, he always buried his mouth and nose in his red-and-white polka dotted handkerchief. Occasionally he risked instant infection by raising his mask a chink to hiss - "More water ... more water ... you're stifling me boy."

In his run-down state of health, Lynch grew cold-rife and constantly monopolised what heat there was from the open fire, even to the extent of turning up the tail of his jacket and pressing his bum against the stout metal fireguard. Another favourite stance was perched on his high stool close against the fireguard, side - on to the scholars.

In the cramped working conditions he couldn't wink without various pairs of eyes resting upon him. The scrutiny was merciless and as his hypochondria increased his antics evoked ribald laughter as soon as the scholars got outside the classroom. He had got into the habit of checking his pulse beat at frequent intervals, inspecting his tongue with the aid of a tiny mirror and swallowing pills from a tin box labelled "Peps". Then he started swallowing eggs straight from the shell. He would stealthily take one from his desk and edge out into the porch with it concealed in the palm of his hand. Generally, he made the mistake of not closing the door fully, in order to hear any noise which the boys might make in his absence. What he didn't bargain for was the ability of Joe Bone or whoever else was at the back near the hinge of the door, to spy on him through the crack and mime his actions as he cracked the egg shell against the jamb of the porch and swallowed the contents. When he re-emerged wiping egg off his moustache with his handkerchief, two score boys had their heads down as one - concentration 100%.

When winter came, he stopped the raw eggs. Instead, a lucky lad called Fonsie McGowan was dispatched daily at 2 pm sharp to fetch an egg flip from Mrs. Bann's house across the road. She was the sexton's wife. The treat arrived piping hot and Lynch swallowed it with relish. God knows he needed it. At that stage he had got so weak he could hardly push his bike and he had had to get unique spring-loaded cranks fitted to the pedals, the like of which had never been seen before. Fortunately he did not know that Fonsie nearly always sipped some of the froth off the egg flip.

Often, the Master confined his secular instructions to basics and took Religious Instruction much more seriously. After all, the parish priest was the school manager. Preparing children for first communion was the Mistress' responsibility but he was apt to butt in, much to her annoyance. The annual visit by Father Walls, the Diocesan Ecclesiastical Inspector, was prepared for well in advance, and Lynch was apt to encroach on time which should have been given to the three Rs., to make sure his boys pleased Father Walls, and that they were saying their prayers, morning and night.

Distrust caused him to dread the first visit by a Ministry of Education School Inspector. School inspectors travelled by horse-drawn "hack cars" in those days and every time such a vehicle came in sight Lynch would get into a flurry. The wall chart inscribed "Religious\Secular Instruction" would quickly be flipped right side out, to correspond with the school timetable, and if the boys happened to be at bible history when they should have been at arithmetic, he would yell ; "Put away those bible history books and open your arithmetic books at page x. Do the first sum on that page. Get out your jotters and pencils this moment before the Inspector comes in."

If, as was mostly the case, the passenger in the hack car was identified through the window at closer range as a "pickie man" (i.e. a credit draper) calling on some of the local residents, the whole procedure was put in reverse right away and study of bible history was resumed.

One day a hack car did indeed bring a Ministry Inspector called Captain Long. Lynch's hostility irked him so much that the good men proceeded to dissect the Master's teaching notes line by line. Then he sat in while lessons proceeded. When it came to geography he quickly spotted the ancient 32-county map of Ireland still in use. It was yellow and cracked like an overripe pea pod and much of it was totally indiscipherable. When some of the boys rhymed off the four provinces of Ireland: Ulster, Munster, Leinster and Connaught and then followed up with Donegal, Londonderry, Antrim, Down, Armagh, Monaghan, Cavan, Fermanagh and Tyrone as the counties of Ulster, Long saw red. He gave Lynch a tongue-thrashing the like of which he had never before had to take. Lynch hadn't a leg to stand on and he knew it. As an ultimatum, Long gave him three months to procure an up-to-date map of Ireland and bring his teaching methods and notes into line - or else! Humiliated and resentful, he was left with no choice but to comply.

All the inmates of country schools were so used to B.O. and worse, as 30 or so unwashed boys dressed in rags, sometimes sodden, crowded in daily, that any kind of a nice smell was bliss, especially if Tommy Trainor, whose foster mother kept a he-goat at stud happened to be dressed in one of his particularly malodourous jerseys. As such times, when the Master was out of earshop, a sibilant hiss "Buck goat ..... Buck goat ..." was the reaction, as classmates moved offside as soon as they could.

The postman rarely visited the school. When he arrived one day with a long brown paper cylinder, tightly parcelled, all eyes were agog to find out what was in it. After glancing at the label, the Master threw it on top of the press (where the new notice board had gone) much to his scholars' chagrin. A few weeks later, just before closing time, they saw him eyeing the thing and frowning. Then, to their delight, he went over to Miss Kelly, borrowed her scissors, lifted down the parcel and began to unwrap it. The pungent smell of varnish mixed with that of new canvas momentarily wiped out the stench of the fetid classroom and as Lynch unfolded a new and gleaming map of Ireland the scholars were elated both by the scent and by seeing something new.

Stretching the map across two desks he traced with his finger the ugly brown line separating the six north eastern counties from the other 26, and explained its significance. Then, his voice breaking with emotion, his solemnly announced, "Now! They have made me an exile in my own country," which of course was Greek to the scholars. Up until then he had been teaching in his native country. Now he felt that partition had marooned him outside, at the mercy of an alien regime.

The Mistress had moved across to view the new map and her pupils crowded around as well. Startled, some of the more observant lads detected tears in the Master's eyes. Solemnly he strode to the corner of the classroom beside the door to the yard, gazed fixedly at the old map of Ireland and then reverently lifted it down, rolled it up, and set it on the top shelf of the high press.

Angrily he barked. "Johnny, fetch that thing to me till I hang it up." Johnny Martin quickly obeyed. Lynch took the new map from the boy and snapped; "Bring over the chair. Get up on it and hang this thing up where the old one was." Johnny nervously did what he was told. As the master straightened it he muttered to himself once more; "Yes; an exile in my own country"

"He started swallowing eggs straight from the shell"

THE EVACUEES

Were there really more long hot days in summer, before the War, or does it seem so because we enjoyed them so much when we were young? There always was great crack around Barton's Bay. The lough shore used to be thronged with townies and we always headed there on our bikes from seven o'clock onwards. The notorious Lough Neagh flies were usually about as well - swarms of them - and we loved to shake a bush just to see them come off it like smoke and envelop the townies.

When rain threatened they were a menace. Riding a bike you could have seen them hovering like low clouds near head level. They were all wings and no bodies, but they would have smarted the eyes out of you. And the more you rubbed, the worse. Often we had to go and pump cold water over our eyes to wash the blighters out.

The townies were nearly as numerous as the flies, relatively speaking. When hot weather drove them out of the wee houses in the working-class Belfast streets they headed for the country in droves - especially the women and children. There were no radios blaring then. The lassies just paraded the road in groups of three or four and there was plenty of larking about but nothing unseemly. Hi mister! Give me a ride on your handlebars," they would shout. Sometimes we did. Sometimes we encouraged them, but as they ran after us we kept moving away, teasing the life out of them. Mostly they were nicely enough spoken, but not all of them. Occasionally, we got a broadside in unprintable Belfast back-street language.

We got to know some of them, at least vaguely. They were too numerous. Where they laid their heads at night was a mystery. Seemingly, they shared out what beds were available on a shift basis. They came year after year, and had their regular lairs but the fisher folk and labourers who lived around Barton's Bay had

11

few spare rooms or spare beds in the hungry thirties. They just roughed it and bedded down anywhere they found space.

There was one tall, fine looking, lassie with auburn hair who was a leader in cadging rides on the bars of bicycles - a real sport and game for a laugh. We only knew her as Molly. She was from somewhere around Carlisle Circus or the Mater Hospital and she used to tell us about her life as a probationer nurse.

When the war came, many things changed. But that time our gang had gone their separate ways and memories of the light-hearted frolics around the Lough of a Summer evening had begun to fade. I started work in the city myself and on the day after the first air raid of 16th April, 1941, I had taken a walk at lunch time as far as the Mater Hospital to see the extent of the damage. Later, when I headed for the station at Great Victoria St., I found hundreds of people assembled in and around the entrance in a stampede out of the city. I had a season ticket and was familiar with the place so I was able to reach the platform, via Glengall St. entrance and get aboard. Outside the ticket barrier, there was a sea of faces. Every inch of space was crowded with desperate folk seeking escape from the nightmare of a city expecting another nocturnal onslaught by Hitler's bombers.

I got home a little late. Train timetables had gone haywire but I was glad to be out of it. When I reached home I got the surprise of my life. Who was there, but Molly. With her was her husband, an Englishman, who was an aircraft factory employee and their two children. One was about three and she told me her name was June. The other was a new-born baby. Like most other folk who had lived through the Hell of the air-raid on Belfast of 15/16th April, they had spent a night on Cave Hill and when morning came they had fled with little more than what they stood up in. They had got a bus to Aghalee, and walked the last mile to our place.

Fortunately we had room, but conveniences in the country then were rather primitive, and poor Molly had neither gas nor electricity to heat the baby's bottle, nor a handy shop to supply essentials. When the second air raid of 5th May hit Belfast, she spent the whole night walking the landing, watching the glare in the sky, 20 miles away and listening to the occasional crump as another landmine exploded. The dull drone of heavy engines continued overhead for hours, and we had difficulty in reassuring our guests that Aghagallon was a long way from Belfast - and safe. Next day when the impact of the terrible happening of that night hit us, we were not quite so complacent. Molly's husband and I had to head off as usual, and Belfast was not a pretty sight on 6th May, 1941, when all the public baths had to be turned into morgues and devastation and acrid yellow smoke were everywhere.

12

"Give me a ride on your handlebars"

ROBBING THE WILD BEES

What have the new-fangled methods of harvesting grass done to our fields and haggards? The stink of silage has replaced the scent of hay, and the corncrake, with its harsh crake, regular as the beat of a metronome, has gone; and with it the fun of trying to spot that elusive Pimpernel. As soon as he says his piece, he darts off with his head well down, to open up with a fresh crake, fifty yards away, head up. So clever was he that, in childhood, we never knew whether there were two corncrakes, or four, in the field of long grass. After sunset, of a May evening, the countryside would have been loud with the monotonous cries of the corncrake, answering each other from one field to another, and echoing in the stillness.

Then there was the white frothy "cuckoo spit," on the hedgerows. Are they still there, I wonder? We really blamed the cuckoo in our innocence.

And what have they done to the clear crystal streams that we drank out of and fished in, as children? They stink now.

Many a happy hour we idled away, lying on our bellies, peering at the spricks in the river between Aghadrumglasny and Ballykeel townlands. There was a disused flax hole at the south-west corner of the meadow bounded by that stream, but I do not remember any flax being grown locally. There was talk of its having been recently abandoned, because it had taken too much good out of the soil, and was too hard to pull.

My memories of that little meadow, the one at the bottom of the sand field, are all happy ones. When I was very young, I trotted along behind the horse-drawn mower, from the moment my father first entered by the gap to cut the first swathe around the perimeter. The weather was usually sultry and the sky overcast, and the clegs would have been driving the horses mad. Every now and then Dad would stop and bash them with his palm, as they crawled over the sweaty necks of the horses. The cattle in the sand field went charging around, like demented things, with their tails up, boring their way through thickets of bramble and sally around the hedges, in an effort to shake off their torturers. The cheeks and necks of the horses became stained red with blood drawn by the clegs, and spread when the insects were squashed. The blood mingled with the sweat, and hairs, and the animals flicked their muscles to dislodge the attackers, jerked their heads, and restlessly pawed the ground. Only years of discipline and schooling prevented them from obeying their natural instincts to take off, like the cattle in the field beside them. Sometimes Dad encouraged us to get a light leafy bough from a sally bush and beat off the insects, as they homed in on the tortured steeds. We got bitten ourselves, in the process, and so did Dad, but retribution was swift. The cleg which homed in to attack seldom survived to bite again.

Older children of the family joined us in the hay meadow, when they came from school, and started hunting on the stubble for wild bees' nests. When they found one, they yanked the top off it with a rake and ran like the wind, pursued by the angry bees. Before attacking the nests, they armed themselves with leafy branches and worked in twos or threes so as to be able to protect one another by beating off the pursuing bees. The aim was to snatch a honeycomb full of honey. More often than not, there was no honey, only maggots in the comb, but occasionally honey was found, and eagerly sucked by the lucky finder. Usually only a few bees were at home - not a swarm. They were mostly out gathering food. Anyone who ever robbed the wild bees' nests in a hay meadow, will appreciate Yeats' reference to "the bee loud glade."

As I grew older, and had to take my place on the team sent to turn the hay in the meadow with wooden hay rakes; life was no longer all fun. The leader, who was older, set a cracking pace, as he skilfully tipped the swathes over with a well-practised jerk of the rake head, always working with the swathe, in the direction in which it had fallen when mowed. That way, the swathe retained its cohesion. Any attempt to work in the opposite direction resulted in the swathe becoming completely fragmented, and unmanageable. Sometimes, when the hay had been turned and the weather was poor, we had to set to work with pitch forks and tease it all up to dry. This was called shaking it.

Given fine weather, the crop would have been ready for putting up into cocks before the end of the day, after turning. The horse-drawn rake would have been brought in, and the hay would have been pulled into ridges across the meadow. Each time the rake filled, a lever was pulled to off-load, then the teeth of the rake were quickly let down again, to repeat the filling process. When all the crop had been ridged, the tumbling Paddy was used to collect the ridges into heaps, at a spot selected as the site for each cock. The operator knew exactly how much hay to assemble for each cock, and he was seldom very far out.

As soon as the hay had been collected the building of the cock was commenced. That was not a job for a lad, but we were given hand rakes and kept busy. When the stack was half completed, we had to crawl in on all fours to trim the base, using our bare hands. That was *not* a pleasure. Work went on in raising the stack and we had to remain on our knees, and pull out all the loose hay around the perimeter of the stack, otherwise, when the stack settled, a lot of hay would have been in contact with the ground, needlessly, and deteriorated in quality, as a result. As we worked, hay and hay-seed rained down on us from the pitchforks of the workers who were throwing hay up to the man standing on the stack, building it.

Trampled stacks were the norm in our particular district. After the stacks were finished, cleaned up, roped, etc., the whole meadow was raked clean with the horse rake and the rakings were added to the final stack, or put in a mini-stack, separate.

As lads, we got more crack when the ruckshifter was brought out, to shift the hay stacks from the meadow to the haggard, where maybe eight of them would have been incorporated in a larger stack, which might have been 25 feet high and nearly as many feet across. These were called packs, locally, and it took a highly skilled man to build them. He walked around on top of the pile of hay forming it into a cone, always keeping the heart well packed, and higher than the edges, so as to throw off the wet. Packs had to weather all the winter storms and in addition to being uprights, with raised cores, they had to be particularly skilfully headed, that is to say, rounded off at the apex, which would have been no larger than the area covered by the soles of the boots of the man who built them. He had to balance there precariously while ropes were slung over the pack and weighted down at the base with lumps of scrap iron. These dangled about four feet from the ground and later, as we played tig around the finished stacks in the haggard, many a bruise we suffered. The only sympathy we ever got was - "You ought to have watched where you were going"!

When the time came to break into a pack of hay it was customary to take a slice off it, vertically, with a hay knife, as a shopkeeper might carve a round of cheese. The roof of the pack was not taken off until room had been found for all the hay in some of the sheds. The hay knife was a wide-bladed instrument with a kind of a T handle.

Once, when my brother John and I had been helping the men to draw in cocks of hay with a ruckshifter, John wakened up in the middle of the night yelling "It is going to split." My father had dashed into the room roused by the commotion, and he immediately responded - "Get the rope over it, quick." At that my sleep-walking brother dived under the bed groping for a rope! He evidently thought he was still out in the meadow alongside the ruckshifter. Hay cocks often "whummeled," that is, split horizontally, when they were being windlassed on to the steeply inclined ruckshifter.

"Beating off the pursuing bees"

THE HIRED BOY

I was just 14, and I had only left school. I hadn't any work, or a penny in my pocket. Times were hard in them days. My mother was having bother keeping me. This man asked me, one day, would I give him a day's work. I said I would, for I badly needed money.

I asked him what I would have to do, and he told me he would show me when I went. "I'll tell you in the morning" was what he said. He had a wee bit of ground in the moss (Montiaghs) and when I went in the morning he said he had corn to harrow. He asked me to take one end of a wee harrow to help him to carry it. It was a wee light seed harrow, with short pins.

I helped him down to the field with it. He had a rein-cord as well, and when we got to the corn-field he tied one end of the rope to the harrow, and gave me the other, which he told me to put over my shoulder. He showed me how to pull it, and where to go. On and off he gave me a hand. We were at it all day. There was about an acre in the plot and we harrowed it all. I was tough at that time. I had had plenty of experience of hard work when I was at school - helping my father to make mud turf and draw them home, and milking, and driving the horse in the cart, and putting the harness on and off him, and things like that. At the end of the day - and it was a long one - he gave me one and six. That would be seven and a half pence now.

When we had nearly finished, my father arrived with another man, a dairy farmer from the Tansy. He had heard I was strong and a good milker, and he had come to hire me. He offered £18 and my keep, for six months' work. My father asked me would I go, and I said I would. The man said he needed a good milker, and I was glad to hear it, for I was a dandy milker. I could have held my own with anyone - and maybe I still could.

I went to him on the Sunday night, that was 11th May 1919. I started next morning - the 12th May. It was about 12 miles from home. I had an old bicycle that cost me thirty shillings, and I was paying sixpence a week off. When I got to the farm at the Tansy, the man was looking out for me. He called his wife out and said - "I want you to meet our new boy." His wife was a very kindly woman. She made me tea, and gave me as much bread as I could eat. When I had finished, the man reached up above his head in the kitchen, and pulled dowm a ladder, which he then set up. Then he climbed up into the loft, and told me to follow him.

It was a lovely snug wee loft, with a nice single bed and things. There was a candlestick and a new candle, and a box of matches. He asked me did I smoke, and when I said I didn't, he said, "That's a good job. If you are lighting the candle be very careful, for you are close to the thatch, and you could put the whole place up in flames." I was *very* careful.

He said; "Your bedtime is half-nine and you will rise at half-five. I'll not call you twice." He had 18 cows, and I had to have the milk at Ballinderry station for the twenty-past-eight train every morning. I took it in a keg, with the horse and cart. It would have been nearly two miles to the station.

Before I went to bed the first night I had a walk around. When I got to the back of the haggard, out of sight, I climbed up a big ash tree to see if I could see home. I went right up to the topmost branch and I was swaying like a bird, but all I could see was Ram's Island and the lough - no home. I cried then, for I had never been away before and I was very lonely.

One day we had to dip the sheep. The man handed me an old shirt before we started and said.

"Give me your shirt and put that one on instead. We have to watch the tics." I did as I was told, and when we had finished I had a good wash before I put my own shirt on again. That night was the only time I lit that candle. I wakened up in the middle of the night with a terrible pain in my oxter. When I lit the candle I couldn't see what it was but I hoked with my thumb nail, and I brought out bits of an insect. I couldn't get it all out, but I stopped the bad pain. Next morning, the man and his wife looked under my arm and they said it was a tic. The woman dosed it with iodine, and I never looked behind me. Wasn't I lucky I didn't get poisoning?

I stayed the six months, but I was homesick the whole time. I used to get home for an hour of a Sunday. We usually quit work about half-six in the evening, and I had nowhere to go, and I knew nobody. I never brought anybody in. I don't think them people would have liked me to have brought anybody about the house. I got the best of food - beef every day nearly - but I never was able to eat much, I was that homesick. I just knocked about the fields, and haggard in the evenings, glad to give a hand with anything to pass the time.

When I left, I never went back. Some people wondered at that for they had been very good to me. Even when I got older and had a motor-bike I never went. I just couldn't go back. I had been that homesick all the time.

After that, I got a job with a farmer at George's Island, but him and me had a dispute over pay. He was giving me fifteen shillings a week and he went to reduce it to twelve. I left. My mother was upset. "What *are* you going to do?" she said. "Where *will* you get another job?" I said; "I don't care. I'm not going to work for that money", nor I didn't.

I got into a basket factory a wee while after that, and I stayed nearly 20 years.

"For I was a dandy milker"

FOXED

The half-door of the squalid mud-walled thatched cabin hung drunkenly on one hinge, and the threshold was bedded with sheaves of straw where the timber of the door had rotted away. A haze of blue peat smoke filled the dingy single apartment, drifting out on the chill air of the November afternoon. In the distance the Mourne mountain range was fast disappearing in the gloaming of an autumn day.

An elderly lady, muffled up in a shapeless shawl, was barely visible in the ill-lighted interior, seated to one side of the hearth on a settle bed and another lady wearing an old tweed coat came to the door as I approached. I identified myself as from the welfare, and explained that I was simply making a friendly call, to find out how they were getting on, and to check that they had got their allowance books and knew how to handle them.

I was invited in cordially but the atmosphere was anything but inviting. I stepped over the straw-lined threshold when the door had been dragged open far enough to let me in. Then I shook hands with both the old ladies. One was blind - the immobile one. Her sister, obviously over 80, looked older.

I had been very curious to see the conditions for myself, as I had had a graphic description from the regular home visitor, Jimmy, newly transferred to the country from Belfast city. I noted the stalactites of soot and tar hanging from the interior rafters of the low, thatched, roof - the fruits of decades of a smoking chimney - also the broken windows, blocked up with sheaves of oat-straw, the onion-case on its side beneath the window. And the unmistable evidence of hens having nesting recently therein, also the feathers and droppings at the foot of the ancient metal bedstead, which stood in the corner of the room, to the left of the cobbled hearth.

I noted that the once whitewashed interior was yellowed with age, and marked with brown water stains from the thatch and the scraw.

I looked for a table, cooking stove or cupboard, but there was none. A rickety wooden dresser and a tea-chest with a battered, loose, lid, and a couple of well-smoked, wooden, butter boxes comprised the remaining furnishings of this crude bed-sitter, which had been home to the family for their entire lifetime.

The year was 1948, and Assistance Board had just recently taken over the relief of need from the Poor Law Guardians. Jenny and Rosie until then had had to exist on a total of sixteen shillings (80p) a week, Jenny, the elder, had had a blind person's pension of ten shillings (50p) and Rosie had had six shillings (30p) by way of Poor Law outdoor relief. They jointly owned the small cabin and the adjoining plot of two acres of useless rocky mountain land. Mercifully, their overheads were virtually nil

They were delighted that the award of National Assistance meant that their struggle to survive had been brought to an end. Now they could look forward to being able to live in comfort, they said, and they were overjoyed with the allowances which had been granted. Repeatedly they expressed this. I promised to see if anything more could be done, and as I took my leave, I explained that Mr Stevenson the man who had visited them on earlier occasions, was outside in the car afraid to venture in, because of what had happened to their fowl. I also added a word of sympathy

They shrugged the whole thing off and asked me to tell "the other man" not to fret; "It didn't matter; he had only done his best. Tell him to come on on in. He is very welcome."

When I got back to the car and gave my colleague, Jimmy Stevenson, the message, he was mightily relieved. The taxi driver, Willie Young, laughed heartily!

What had happened was this. Jimmy, a city-bred zealot, had taken his responsibility for the welfare of the client very seriously, and when he had found these two old dears sharing their living quarters with their hens, he had set out to persuade them to behave in a more civilised manner, going so far as to enlist the support of the canon. Jenny and Rosie had eventually been persuaded to re-house the hens in a crude shelter of sticks and sods, constructed in a corner of the garden behind the cabin.

When I had decided to accompany Jimmy on his daily rounds this had been one of the cases which I had asked to be included. En-route Willie Young, the taxi driver, had learnt that a marauding fox had cleared out Jenny and Rosie's hen coop. Jimmy had taken cold feet and persuaded me to let him opt out when we had arrived at the old ladies' cabin..

"A marauding fox had cleared out the hen coop"

WHEN ONE DOOR CLOSES

Little Miss Morrison felt safe. Nobody could see her as she lurked in her gloomy hallway. In common with all the neighbours, her door lay wide open. She loved to watch for the commuters coming off the quarter-past six. They nearly all took the far side of the street, which was sunny, and passed in small groups. She knew most of them by sight and many of them by their first names, through travelling in the same coach with them for years. Not that she had socialised with them. She had always kept to herself.

When old Mr. Johnston, who had the High Street shoe shop passed, she realised it was Wednesday. He always went to the wholesalers on early closing day. She hadn't had a caller from Monday morning when the rent man had been and she hardly knew what day it was. She was glad to know it was Wednesday, for she was out of vegetables - the man would be round with some on Thursday.

The sight of the three young girls from Newell's passing by cheered her up. She saw that the red-headed one had a lovely shade of green on her today - green with white polka dots - and she went to her window for a closer look.

It was like the blue cotton dress that she had seen in Newell's window last summer, she thought, the one she had kept an eye on for nearly a week. When she had got her pay and hurried round, it had been sold. She had felt like cursing Mason's and their miserly wages. Only for that she could have got it when she saw it first. They had been a lot more open-handed when they had been coaxing her to retire early, but what good was the money to her now, when she had nowhere to wear good clothes. She remembered how the senior saleslady in Newell's had tried to console her by remarking that maybe the blue dress had been a bit young in style, and that if she waited, a more matronly model would probably come in. If only she had had better pay she would have been able to have had more nice clothes, she mused.

The appearance of "the four big men" diverted her thoughts. She knew their first names, since they had used them all the time on the train. She liked the one called Ted best. He was friendly. The sandy-haired one, called Trevor, was always sneering at people, and she didn't like him at all. The other two, Peter and Andy, were quiet, and she had not quite made up her mind about them. She thought she saw Trevor looking in and she retreated into her living-room.

She had no way of knowing that the four men had been discussing her as they passed. They knew all her peculiarities and they had carefully avoided glancing her way. At least all of them did, except Trevor.

"There's that oul doll Morrison, again. She's like a big thrush under a garden hedge on a wet day, with that haystack of clothes and the oul scarf round her head. She'll need an operation to get her three coats off," he scoffed.

Ted just remarked quietly; "It's a pity of her. She is obviously very lonely from the way she stands there looking out at people passing."

"D'ye mind how she used to prowl up and down the train, trying to avoid smoke?" Trevor went on. "Mason's had to get rid of her. She was stinking with B.O. Not a damned bit of wonder. Even when it was about 80 degrees in the train, she had fur boots on, and three coats, and that oul muffler around her head."

"I hear her brother from Craigavad hardly ever comes near her," Trevor went on. "She never goes out, except once a fortnight. Sure she travelled daily for about a year after Masons gave her the push. She wanted the neighbours to think that she was still working. Tom Moffett told me she spent every day in the Linenhall Library, and then came home as usual on our train."

Trevor's fellow travellers let the subject drop. There was no point in contradicting Trevor. It only made him more dogmatic.

Ted resolved to go over and speak to the old soul if she ever gave him an opening. Some evenings later, when he had called at the newsagents, he was behind his mates, and he took the other side of Hill Street. As he passed Morrison's he glanced in and caught Miss Morrison's eye. She smiled wanly, so he said; "Good evening", and kept on walking.

About a week later he was alone again and he repeated the exercise. This time he deliberately paused and inspected the 'busy Lizzie' plant in her window, but again he walked on. He was aware that she had been watching him intently, but he decided not to say anything. Instead, he left it until a later occasion. Again he stopped to inspect the plant. Then he remarked:

"That's a real beauty. I can't get them to grow like that. You must have green fingers."

As he had hoped, Miss Morrison's face immediately lit up and she began an animated account of the knack of propagating 'busy Lizzie' pot plants, ending up with an offer to provide him with a cutting. Her words bubbled forth like the waters of a stream from which a dam had just been removed, and he instantly realised that he had found the key. He encouraged her to talk and promised to bring a pot for the promised cutting.

When he went back he carried a bunch of beautiful red tulips from his wife's garden. Miss Morrison was estatic. Gently she traced the contours of the delicate blooms with her wizened, and none-too-clean, fore finger, totally enraptured. It was easy to establish a friendly relationship after that. Ted brought his wife one day and afterwards they regularly kept in touch by calling as they passed.

They were never invited in until the following spring, when Miss Morrison unexpectedly asked advice about a hydrangea plant. It emerged that she had one 'at the back' which wasn't thriving and she proceeded to guide them on a tour of her tiny, and quite pathetic, flowergarden in the corner of her backyard. A glance at the arid soil was sufficient. Obviously the plants were suffering from starvation, not only root starvation, but absence of light in the grimy soot-laden corner behind the perimeter wall.

As kindly as possible they explained that poor soil and insufficient light were hampering growth and that possibly a complete change of soil was the only remedy. Fertilisers were discussed, and it was left that Miss Morrison would try Wellworths the next time she was up the town. It was she who mentioned that. They both knew she *never* went further than the post office and shop at the end of Hill Street, but out of kindness they let her have her bout of wishful thinking. Or was it, perhaps, a little bit of subterfuge? Anyhow, a couple of weeks later they fetched her a bag of fertiliser saying they had been getting some for their own use. She insisted on their accepting the last penny which it had cost.

From time to time, when encouraged, she mentioned some littled need. Sometimes a packet of salt. Maybe a box of matches. They were happiest when she let them bring her something. Occasionally, at set times, they brought her a tasty dish, passing it off as her share of a birthday party, which they had had, or something special. In this way, they got her round to accepting a Sunday lunch.

One day they found her depressed and tearful. It emerged that she had long been annoyed by mice and that now they had become a big problem.

"They are even in my bed, and I hate them," she confided. Ted brought a trap but she explained that it would be useless.

"They are all over the place. There must be a dozen," she moaned. A cat was suggested but she dismissed the idea,

"Too dirty."

She wanted poison and although Ted warned her of the likelihood of bad smells if any died under the floor boards, she was insistent, so they undertook to fetch some.

On the way home Ted remarked to his wife, Mary, that he supposed another smell would hardly be noticed. Mary laughed, for indeed Miss Morrison's abode did not smell too sweet. Of course, they would never have said so to any third party. They felt heart sorry for the old lady. Juniper Terrace, where she lived had originally been the residence of lower middle class folk with the working class people all in the smaller kitchen houses down the street. The Morrisons had always been people of substance and Miss Morrison was a gentle soul.

Ted brought her the poison and much to his delight it worked. As well, she escaped the smell of carcases under the floorboards - which was a mini-miracle. The old lady was very, very happy to be rid of the pests and kept thanking them profusely for weeks afterwards.

As winter wore on, Miss Morrison began to go downhill fast. Sometimes, when they called for the crockery after they had left a meal it hadn't been washed - which was totally unusual, for she was very very fastidious. Once or twice they twigged that she had hardly touched the food.

Coming up to Christmas they arranged delivery of dinner on Christmas Day. As usual, Miss Morrison was profuse in her thanks. Christmas fell on Saturday and on the Wednesday previous Ted dropped a Christmas card in Miss Morrison's letter box with a note on it which read:

"See you at 2.30 Saturday, with Christmas dinner. Happy Christmas!"

He had been pushed for time, so he hadn't rung the bell. On Christmas Day he arrived with the meal at 2.30 pm sharp. He left his ten-year-old daughter nursing the tray in the car while he rang Miss Morrison's bell. Twice he rang it, but each time there was no response.

Just then, a next-door neighbour arrived in his car, with several children. When he saw Ted at the door he shouted.

"There's nobody in."

Ted immediately responded.

"She's in all right. She is slow to open the door. She has to have a look first."

"I tell you there's nobody in," the neighbour retorted a bit testily. "She is dead."

Ted froze.

"Miss Morrison isn't dead! She couldn't be"

"She is", the neighbour replied. "Her brother got her lying in the hall on Wednesday evening dead. She had a card in her hand, apparently the only one she had got."

"She loved to watch the commuters coming off the quarter-past-six"

A POOR MAN IN NEED OF HELP

Anthony Patrick Lowry, to give him his full and preferred style of address, was a strolling beggar - the type who might have got a badge permitting him to go from house to house within his native parish if he had been born in the eighteenth, instead of the nineteenth, century. But he was neither a beggarman nor a tramp in his own estimation - but just "a poor man in need of a wee bit of help," and he carried no badge.

He was an irascible character with an irrepressible flow of invective when roused, which was not infrequent. There was no surer way of having a row and a ruction than to allude to him as a beggar or a tramp in his presence, or to address him by his nickname of "Anthony Duck", or "Tony."

Every schoolboy in the parish took delight in provoking him, and some of the menfolk were not far behind them. As a local he enjoyed the freedom of every working class house in the parish of Kilmore, where doors were left on the latch night and day, but he was a pest to housewives on account of his endless shopping list and his persistent soliciting. He carried a jute bag slung over one shoulder and spent his time filling this - mostly with old clothes, pieces of bread wrapped up in newspapers, tea, sugar, milk etc. When one bag was full, he stacked it in one of his many lairs, and brought out another .... a real jackdaw in his habits.

One afternoon he made his way up Sally McCrory's loanen looking forward to a rest by her fireside. It was pouring rain and he was in a bad mood.

His stay was short, very short, and when he headed back down the lane he had a scowl on his face and his chin thrust forward. A briar with the talons of an eagle whipped his cap off and when he retrieved it, he cursed the briars into hell, and slashed at them with his hazel cudgel, as he slithered and stumbled over the water-logged surface and headed for the tarred road.

The unthinkable had happened. That young whippersnapper Barney McCrory had sacrilegiously laid hands on him and flung him out of McCrory's - a house where he had always been treated kindly, even before he had taken to the road with a bag on his back.

"Since he got that job at Stormont, licking aul Craigavon ass, he thinks he can walk over everybody," Anthony muttered. "When I get him to Crumlin for assault and damage to my property he'll know where he is. Aul Craigavon. A Renegade!" With Crumlin Courthouse in mind, Anthony began rehearsing what he would tell the Sergeant.

"I was just a poor man needing a bit of help and doing nobody any harm. I was sitting there minding my own business in his mother's house when he lit on me and assaulted me, and threw my bag out into the clabber, and used abusive language and insults ... I had lifted the latch and went in, as usual. Sally had bread on the griddle and she was minding that and washing the dishes at the same time. She had no complaint, but that ignorant gulpin of a son of hers just glowered at me. He had his nose in a book as usual, filling his head with big ideas.

Sally put on the tea drawer and gave me a mug of tay and some loaf bread. When I had it ate I gave her my wee milk bottle an' she scoured it and filled it for me. Then I asked her for a wee bit of bread and I got that - an' a wee grain of tea and a lock of spoonfuls of sugar. She made wee pokes for them out of newspaper and I asked for the rest of it as I hadn't seen a paper for a good while

It was when I asked her for a wee 'dout' of a candle that they both got nasty. Sally ate the face off me and told me she had no candles and where did I expect her to get candles ... and that kind of thing. I knowed rightly she had candles - hadn't I seen them - and I told her so. I maybe said she was a scrooge ... Anyhow, that's when *he* started shouting at me to get out. I told him it was his mother's house and had no business .... but before I even got time to get on my feet he had me by the coat collar an' trailed me across the kitchen - and opened the dure an' pushed me out. Then he went back and threw my bag out after me,.... and damaged all my property ... an' broke my milk bottle an' ...

Anthony was that busy planning that he forgot what time it was or where he was and he never looked sideways passing Kilmore School. But he soon wakened up. He wasn't more than 50 yards past when he heard the war cry ...

"Anthony Duck ... Anthony Duck ... Anthony Duck ... Ha! Ha! Ha!, Duck! Duck! Duck!" (The scholars were out! He recognised young Morgan's voice. He was always at it.) As he turned on his heel and charged down the road flailing with his stick the scholars were round him like a swarm of bees darting in and out and chanting ... He got a whack at one or two when others pushed them but they were too many for him and he just had to give up and head for Bann's.

Jim was the Sexton and as soon as Anthony opened his door, and him roaring like a bull, Jim jumped out past him and went for the scholars, who were still at it outside the gate. They soon scrammed when Jim appeared and started calling their names and telling them they would hear more about it when he had had a word with Father McKillop.

As soon as the school boys were out of sight,Anthony grabbed his bag and his stick and marched off towards the school. His big flat boots went flailing up and down, and out, like a duck's webbed feet as he darted along, here's me head and me ass is coming, sort of style and the tail of his jute sack kept bobbing about above his bum. "Oh Anthony Duck all right," Jim muttered, "Well named."

Master Galvin was about to get on his bike when he heard Anthony bellowing at him, "Ach no! Not again", Galvin thought. But yes, indeed it was "again". Before he got within 20 yards range, Anthony started his litany. The master know it all by heart.

... A poor man ... not doing anybody any harm ... just minding his own business ... can't get walking the county road ... etc, etc, etc.

Galvin was in a hurry and also very tired telling Anthony that he nearly as bad as the boys, who only wanted to get chased, and that if he would ignore them they would soon leave him in peace. He knew he might as well talk to the wall so he restrained himself and just heard Anthony out in silence, or a least comparative silence: he made occasional sympathetic noises. When Anthony had cleared his stomach he picked up his belongings and shuffled off.

He cooled off a bit after that and he began to have doubts about going to the barracks. Sergeant Russell was a very ignorant man - no manners at all. When he had gone to him a fortnight ago about Rabbie Geddis and Ned burning his property that he had stored in their potato house, Russell had taken their side. They had accused him of bringing rats about the place, with his old bags stuffed with blue-moulded bread and cheese and bacon and them kind of thing. Nobody took any heed of the good boots and shirts and things. He recalled that he had threatened Russell with aul Dawson Bates, the Minister of Home Affairs. Russell had told him not to come back, ... maybe it would be a bit soon yet?

He discovered blood when he wiped the back of his neck with his pocket handkerchief, thinking it was sweat. That was McCrory's aul briars, he realised. "It would suit that lazy bugger better if he would get up off his ass and take a hook and clear up his mother's loanen," he muttered. He would tell him that to his face some day when there was plenty of people listening.

He had a lair up Rock Lane, at Tommy Teuton's farm. A bed of straw in the corner of the byre suited him fine. When he got there it was dark and there was a bicycle at the door that he recognised as John Heaney's. Heaney was always annoying him by offering to get him work and openly accusing him of being too lazy to take it. That was a very sore spot, possibly because there was some truth in it. Anyhow, he didn't go into Teuton's house but passed on to the byre where he bedded down.

He hadn't been there long when Teuton and Heaney came in with a hurricane lamp and began to discuss the condition of one of the animals which was at the point of calving. Her pelvic bones were felt and she was monitored to see if she was sick or still chewing the cud. It went on and on, and on, till Anthony could thole it no longer, so he chimed in. As soon as he opened his mouth, Heaney spun around and quipped; "Will ye put your head down Anthony, and keep quiet. Do you want the cow to look round and think she has calved a ragman."

Anthony's bellow was enough to make a cow abort, but Heaney just guffawed. Anthony then spewed out a terse genealogical piece about the Heaney breed, highlighting the names of all the rogues and vagabonds of past generations. That made Heaney guffaw even more. A truce set in after that and Heaney and Teuton took themselves off.

In a couple of day's time, tired of all the annoyance he was getting, Anthony decided to move on to Kilwarlin; "Where a body might get a bit of peace." With Winter coming on he had a mind to get out his donkey and cart. Ned Carr was grazing the animal for him.

He had very little road sense and the donkey had less, and when he was dawdling along the broad road near Trimmery one night after dark with no tail light except the wee red pane in the back of the cart-lamp, some fellow in a motor car drove into him and smashed the cart. The donkey survived and so did Anthony. He'd been walking alongside, fortunately, and escaped with bruising and a broken leg.

He was taken to Waringfield Hospital where he lay for weeks - a bit of a thorn in the sides of the nurses but one which they confessed they enjoyed because of his irascible nature and colourful language about "the eejit that smashed his ass' cart."

He had been there a long time and having a lonely time when, one evening, who should drop in to see him but Barney McCrory from the St Vincent de Paul Society. Anthony welcomed him like a long lost brother.

"How are ye Barney. I am glad to see you! And how's your good mother? A kind, decent woman ... You will tell her I was asking for her and that I'll be round to see her as soon as they let me out of this place ..."

"Aul Craigavon", and all the "renegade" taunts that he had thrown at Barney were forgotten. There wasn't even a word about the briars.

Barney was speechless as he gazed at the genie in the bed who had emerged from the midden of frowsy top coats, shaggy locks and smelly unwashed body known as 'Anthony Duck'. His surprise showed, and the more it grew the wider Anthony's grin became. Barney's eyes took in the name card ANTHONY PATRICK LOWRY and he recognised Anthony's dictation. He was sorely tempted to stretch across and add "LLD."

"Just a poor man in need of a wee bit of help"

33

A MAN OF CONSEQUENCE

When the commuters dropped their bicycles willy nilly around the platform of Killymun station and dashed for the 7.00 am train, as the guard blew his whistle impatiently, William Wilson was just "Wee Billie," hail-fellow-well-met. When he dashed off the train and onto Great Victoria Street, to spring on to the tailboard of one of the Queen's Island trams queueing there, he was just a nondescript workman in greasy overalls and duncher cap. Like everyone clinging to the brass rail on the tailboard, he was insignificant and anonymous.

It was the same at the other end, but inside the shipyard gate he became a board number. To "the hat," as they dubbed the foremen in the Yard, he wasn't worth a second glance - unless, of course, he stepped out of line. William seldom did that. Billie's foreman behaved as if he were the Lord God Almighty, and Wee Billie knew he was lucky that he had got staying on. The last big pay-off had had him uneasy, in spite of reassurance that he had been given, through the "old boy" network. "They" had got him in after the war, and he hoped they would have enough pull to make sure that he didn't get his cards. Although he was only a five-eights, as a caulker, a job was a job, with nearly 12 years service he thought he had done all right. Anyhow, he was determined to keep his head down, and not give "the hat" any excuse to find fault.

At home he had a good-looking and loving wife, and a lovely family. He was "Willie" to Rose, and of course, "Da" to the girls. In the closely-knit local community, he was able to hold his head high but he loathed the familiar "Billie" tag. He owed nobody a ha'penny, and his wife ranked as the best housewife in the parish and kept the place always shining. The one big snag was his squalid thatched cabin, with only oil lamps and no running water, or anything like that - and nothing but a coal fire for cooking, which gave Rose a hard time. The fact that all the local working-class people were in the same boat, except the roadmen, who had council cottages, with slated roofs, and houses in better repair, did not really make the old cabin any easier to stick. Even to have a big fire was a danger, with the thatched roof.

William only got a boost for his ego, when the brethern turned out to walk, in their dark suits, regalia and bowler hats. When he put his hat on, he felt as good as the bucko in the yard, where a bowler hat was the badge of rank of foreman. The fact that, as "Brother William," he had held some sort of office in the local lodge almost from his initiation, helped his morale. His father (now deceased) had been Worshipful Master and William had always been looked up to by the brethren as a kind of heir-apparent. There was no "Billie this," or "Billie that" in the lodge. He was "Brother William" and proud to bear the name "The Glorious Pious and Immortal Defender of the Faith" that the lodge was called after - "LOL 1787 Sons of William." When Brother William marched behind that banner he was a somebody.

He behaved accordingly, at lodge meetings. He knew every rule in the manual, and whether it was a matter of discipline, procedures, or regalia he kept everybody in line. In fact, he was a bit of a martinet, and even before he got on to the Standing Committee those on it had to take notice of what he had to say. As a model Orangeman, William had steadily risen through the ranks, and by 1930 he was Deputy Master, just one step from the top. At 50, he was younger than his dad had been when he had got to the top, but he was impatiently counting the days.

Even as D.M. he was very much ashamed of his old house, but it was cheap, as he acted as a kind of caretaker for the farmer who owned it - a man called Joe Lavery, one of the other sort, but none the worse on that account, always ready to milk the cows for any neighbour who wanted a day out on the 'twelfth' and that kind of thing. Joe was a bit lackadaisical, like all of his kind. His place always lacked what the brethren identified as "the Protestant look," that little bit of extra attention to style and appearances, which they regarded as so essential.

Joe knew about Billie's discontent, and had promised to give the place a face-lift, but he was slow to get around to it. Billie had managed to get him to bestir himself and whitewash the walls in June, but the windows and doors hadn't been touched, and the chimneys and the street were a mess. With the 'twelfth' only weeks away, Billie was definitely getting worked up.

Matters came to a head when an unforeseen turn of events found him installed as Master before the month ended. The joy it brought was immediately clouded by the realisation that his house was a disgrace and would now come under close inspection, since he had, by tradition, to extend hospitality to the members of the lodge on the 'twelfth' morning. As well, it was close to the road, half-way between the Orange hall and station where the lodge would be walking to embark for the Field.

He went after Joe Lavery immediately, and he was really chuffed by the way Joe took the good news. His congratulations were as hearty as any member of the lodge and he seemed genuinely delighted, but as the days passed, and no progress was being made with exterior decoration, Billie's patience got very thin.

It was not until 10th July that Joe really got going, and when the 11th dawned, there was still far too much to be done. Joe brought in his two teenage sons, Ned, aged 18 and Tom, who was a couple of years younger, and work began in earnest. Joe gave the woodwork a coat of purple paint, (Billie's choice) and Ned mounted a ladder to do-up the chimney. Tom did anchorman on the ladder. As soon as Ned laid a hand on the chimney, a loose brick shifted, revealing a tongue of soot protruding like an ass's lug from the tip of the masonry. Being full of devilment, he immediately got an urge to chuck it down on to the hearth and startle Billie, whom he visualised   as having his head up the chimney polishing the crane and crooks which hung over the hearth.

He shouted down to Tom.

"Hi! Boy! - See if there is anything on the fire?" He had in mind any pan, or griddle or other cooking utensil.

Tom darted indoors and shouted back - "No! ˙Why?"

Ned didn't take time to reply. Instead, he flicked the donkey's lug with the trowel. The chinmey was loaded with soot, not having ben swept, but the result was totally unexpected and catastrophic. A barrowful of soot went down!

In a flash, Billie emerged from the doorway, enveloped in soot and ashes, roaring like a bull. Rose was on his heels, in an even worse state, weeping. When Billie looked up, and saw Ned grinning, he nearly went berserk. (The lad couldn't help it as William looked a sorry sight) Mouthing a string of expletives, quite unbecoming a W.M., he made a dart to mount the ladder to chastise the miscreant, but, fortunately, Joe got there in time to stop him. Billie continued to curse and damn accusing Ned of b---- bigotry, because it was the 'twelfth'. But Ned strenuously denied throwing anything down the chimney, and glibly claimed that it was a loose brick, which had moved when he put his hand on it to steady himself. He held up another detached brick, for all to see.

This eventually placated Billie and Rose. Gradually, sanity prevailed and with the arrival home of William's girls from school, teamwork was commenced. The whole interior walls had to be washed down, and redecorated with limewash. Every utensil and ornament on the dresser and elsewhere had to be washed as well. It was a mammoth task, but by nightfall the normal pristine condition of Rose's kitchen-cum-livingroom had been restored. Billie had had to go to the hall to finalise arrangements for the walk on the 'twelfth' morning, but when Joe volunteered to go to the village pub for some of what Billie needed to treat the brethren, good relations were cemented.

On the twelfth morning, when William, resplendent in his bowler hat and the regalia of W.M., ceremoniously led the brethren, he was a very proud man. "Wee Willie" no more!

"Billie emerged enveloped in soot and ashes"

HORSE SENSE

As he contentedly munched away at the ditch back, old Jack never had it so good. A newly-arrived young bay mare was now paired with Robin pulling the potato digger and Jack was only being called on when there was a full cart to be taken to the potato house for emptying, and the boss never hurried at that. Instead, he usually lit up his pipe and strolled alongside with the reins tied to the forebar. Jack knew exactly what to do.

Sometimes the wee cub got driving (or thought so). Jack was sagacious enough to ignore his orders and jerking of the reins.

Young Ned, at 18, had taken over and it was all go, but often it was a case of the more haste the less speed. Things had come to a head at the ploughing. Ned hadn't mastered his father, William's knack of prising the ploughshare out at the end of the furrow by placing his left buttock on the plough handle, leaving his hands free. Robin and Jack automatically swung round, clockwise, pivoting the plough, and took their places for the return furrow. All the boss had had to do was to lift his weight off the handle.

When Ned first took over, he ploughed lumps out of the headrig and blamed the horses. A welt here and a welt there with the rein cord was his idea of schooling. Robin had a short fuse and once his temper was riz he couldn't be handled. Feet were trampled, shoes pulled off and time was wasted. Fortunately Ned was able to replace a cast shoe, otherwise half-a-day would have been wasted.

Recurrent bouts of Fersey had left Jack with stiff joints. He was no longer able to keep out from under Robin's feet when the latter's temper was raised. The more Ned chastised, the less co-operation he got. Eventually, the lad had insisted that Jack would have to be replaced, and his father had acquiesced.

As odd-job-horse Jack was happy to be back in William's hands. The bond forged between them had been very close ... some would have said the horse had sixth sense. Certainly he also had bad habits - particularly a mulish determination to do his own thing, such as turning prematurely, or putting his head down to graze while turning at the end of a furrow. Ned found Jack incorrigible.

The boss also had his own idiosyncracies. Journeys between home and the out farm and to and from town each Friday, were leisurely. When a neighbour hailed William, old Jack immediately stopped, and often the neighbour had a message. William wasn't very literate but he had a mind like a microchip. No wee bits of paper were needed. For his elderly neighbours he provided a wonderful service.

In the fall the pair made their last trip together. It was a bright October evening with a touch of frost. The men were busy at the potatoes, but the funeral of a near neighbour had required William's attendance. The aroma of freshly-turned soil mixed with the tang of broken stalks pervaded the potato plot. A goods train could be heard labouring up Beckett's Hill. "I think - I - can - do it, I think - I can - do it, I think - I -can - do it," it seemed to say. As it topped the rise and ran chortling downhill towards town, the note abruptly quickened, "I knowed - I - could - do it. I knowed - I - could - do it ... do - it - - do it do it -" The frost amplified the sound so that it seemed to come from the next field instead of from a mile distant.

Kerr's Pinks glistened in the fading rays of the sun and the gatherers were working hard, anxious to finish before the light failed. Hardly a glance was thrown at the horse and trap as old Jack leisurely made his way past. He headed for the coach house, stood a while, got impatient and moved to the haggard. William's wife, Mary, had seen the equipage pass the window twice and went out to investigate.

"Go quick and get Ned and them," she shouted to wee Danny "Your Dad has been taken bad."

When the others reached her, Mary was seated in the trap quietly weeping. The boss had suffered a stroke, but faithful to the end, old Jack had fetched him safely home.

In the commotion, the old horse stood for an hour totally neglected. Even when he did all he had to do, no one came near him. He moved away to a water butt, then to the side of a haystack and started to feed.

Eventually, Ned led Jack back to the coach-house and unhitched him. He was free at last and he quickly made his way into the wee green to graze.

From then on, he had many drivers. When he stopped at the sound of a neighbour's voice as they travelled along, he promptly got a jerk of the bit and a flick of the reins. The neighbours didn't mind. They hadn't much in common with the younger set.

Mary took over the feeding and watering of the horses every morning, but Jack never knew who would be driving him. He hated John or Bill coming to put the harness on him. They were unable to fasten the girth of the straddle without nipping his belly and they bruised his mouth as well with the bit when they put the winkers on him in an awkward fashion. Sometimes he dropped his head and marched out of the stable door on them. They had to climb up on the manger to put the strap over his ears and he loved to leave them stranded.

At times he led them a dance by simply keeping a couple of paces ahead as they strove to corral him.

As the years passed, times changed and jaunts to town became infrequent. No longer was there simply a basket of eggs and another of butter to barter for groceries. Larger scale poultry farming had begun, with incubators, brooders and poultry arks. William Stavenson began calling weekly with a motor-van to collect eggs by the case. Davy Thompson the Lisburn meal merchant-cum-grocer also began calling to take an order for poultry feed and groceries. The cubs had all grown up, and eventually a Fordson tractor and an old banger of a motor car took the place of the horses.

The young mare, Jessie developed ring bone prematurely and in spite of the very considerable skill of Bob Napier the local blacksmith, who made slippers and rockers, and all kind of unique shoes, she had eventually to be put down.

Robin and Jack were both put out to graze. Horses had become too slow for the rising generation but both were kept for sentimental reasons, since it was intended that they should end their days in comfort.

One day Jack had been taken to the vet to have the stumps of his teeth levelled. When he was brought home he was let loose in the upper field and kicked up his heels as he galloped towards the gap into the meadow beyond. He never saw the newly-erected strands of barbed wire and took a heavy fall. He got his head up and one foreleg under him, but his other foreleg wouldn't function.

Tom had witnessed his fall and he raced towards him, only to freeze when he saw Jack's inability to rise. He ran for help and soon the old horse was the centre of a huddle of doleful neighbours, one more knowledgeable than the other. All were unanimous in their opinions that the leg was broken and that Jack would have to be put down. James Yarr, Aghalee's sagacious parish horse-doctor was hurriedly fetched, but he too agreed. There seemed nothing for it but to fetch the knacker.

Tom set off on his bike and Scullion, the Lurgan knacker, with his horse-drawn cart with a long metal tail board, was on his heels when he got back. He was no mean judge of horses and as he surveyed Jack's huge frame and shining coat he recognised a goodly prize. But there was more concern and compassion in the man than greed and before he loaded his humane killer he examined and re-examined every inch of Jack's foreleg and shoulder. Again and again he expressed doubt. Finally, he replaced the gun in its holster and said, "I wouldn't put that horse down without a vet. His shoulder is out but I can't find any break. Get Thompson."

The local horse judges all fell silent, respecting Scullion's legendary reputation. No one dared question his opinion, since Jack's fate was at stake.

The cost of a vet was significant but Ned did not hesitate. "Will you ask Thompson to come out?" he said to Scullion. "With a heart and a half, Ned! I'll be surprised if he doesn't bring you good news."

Thompson arrived before the day was out. Like Scullion, he carried out a careful and thorough inspection.

"We'll have to get him indoors," he said. "Have you a slipe? I'll give him a jab to knock him out."

Quickly Ned got Robin, hitched him to the slipe used for moving heavy farm machinery, and brought the equipage alongside old Jack, now laid out unconscious. With the ample manpower available they soon rolled him on to the slipe.

"Fetch him into the hayshed," the vet ordered, "under that beam. That's it! I'll not be long till I'm back."

Thompson kept his word and in an hour or two he had old Jack comfortable slung up to take the weight off the injured shoulder. Then he manipulated the joint and put it in place.

"Keep him warm and give him warm drinks," he ordered, "but don't overdo it. I'll be back in ten days or so."

When he came back and released Jack, the old nag cautiously and very slowly gave a limp - then another and another. "He'll hobble a good while," Thompson remarked, "but it won't hurt. (His working days are over.)"

Old Jack survived for several years but eventually, *sans* teeth, *sans* sight and stiff in every joint, the inevitable had to be faced.

One sunny day as he lay on the brow of the river, unable to lift his head, Scullion had to be recalled. None of the family stayed around. When the knacker's footfalls stirred the grass, the old horse twitched his ears. Gently Scullion took him by the muzzle and turned up the white star on his forehead. His assistant rammed the metal tailboard close in against the carcase. Only the clanking of a windlass broke the stillness

"The Kerr's Pinks glistened in the fading rays of the sun"

WHIPPING THE CAT

I served my time to the tailoring in the nineteen-twenties with my father and grandfather. They worked together. My uncle Joe was there too until he joined up. He was killed in the war. That was the World War. Joe was able to make a pair of men's trousers in a day, all handsewn which was a great day's work in them days, a record. My sister, Rose, helped us after school and later on she got a job with a shop up the town.

My grandfather was old fashioned. He never machined anything; all hand done. He said he didn't believe in them mechanical things. He had been a tailor out in the country before he moved into a house in the town. The house he got was beside a big one owned by a linen lord, who had a great big garden at the back, with fruit trees and a greenhouse and all his orders. Many's the time me and other lads "fogged" his orchard. We used to pinch the apples from the police barracks as well. When we climbed on top of their garden wall we were able to reach the apple tree branches.

When grandfather first started up he used to go out to customers as well as them coming to him. A farmer, maybe one with a son or two, would have got the makings of a suit, or more than one. They bought their own suit lengths in those days. Then they would have sent for Grandad. He would have taken an apprentice with him. The lad carried "the goose" and the lap board, that's the board they did the pressing on. When Grandad would have been sewing there for a while, at the farmer's house, somebody else would have heard about it and maybe sent for him to go to him. The tailors called this "whipping the cat."

There were what were called tramp tailors in the old days. Some of them were from Keady and other faraway places. They would have dropped in looking for a day's work, or more. Most of them were "drooth" men. All they wanted was the money for beer. When the day's work was finished they would have said "We want our money now." Once they got it you mightn't have seen them again for many's the long day. They headed for Paddy Murphy's pub or the Foresters as soon as they got paid. They got about fifteen shillings (75p) a day and porter was cheap, about tuppence a bottle.

In the older days the cloth was altogether different. Mostly, it was navy blue serge or shipcord. Grey or green whipcord. Then there was moleskin as well. You couldn't have worn whipcord out, and the moleskin was even tougher. It was very very heavy stuff. When you had a pair of trousers made you could have stood them up. Then there were a few tweeds and checks and a heavy-grade pilot cloth. The fishermen went in for that. They got coats made of it with velvet collars. I mind sewing on the buttons for my grandad when I started first.

In my young days there was a lot of navy-blue, indigo blue - serge. Navy blue suits were the whole go. At first it used to turn green when it faded. You could have seen how bad it was when a fella turned up his coat collar in rain. We hadn't the secret of the dye but that was one thing the Germans had to hand over after the first war. That ended it all. The coats used to turn green round the shoulders and the collars with the old dye.

It was nearly all cut-make-and-trim. Customers brought their own suit - lengths to be made up. They got measured. Then the suit was cut out, the linings were cut and all the parts for the trousers and the jackets and waistcoats were parcelled up, all separate. The buttons and pockets the waistbands and things like that. All the parts were packed up and laid out separately, with the canvas and other trimmings.

The tailor would have basted the stuff on Tuesday for the first fit on of a Tuesday night. Then on Wednesday morning it would have all been ripped out again and the linings and things would have been cut out, and the cido. Special heavy canvas interlinings were used for the collars and lapels - horse hair stiffening material and black linen for putting down the front of jackets, or light grey for light suits. We called the interlinings "cido." All the interlinings were got from Cliftons of Rosemary St. Belfast. They had a big warehouse.

Some other tailors in the town did tailoring for the draper's shops. I wrought for a while for one oul boy who was a tarra for the drink. They called him "The Whacker". When he went on the beer about proper, the shops couldn't get their suits off him. Then when he came off the binge, or the money was done, he might have taken a notion and started at 12 o'clock on a Sunday night and wrought to morning to get the suits finished for Tuesday. Tailors never worked on a Monday.

He was a Holy Terror. He never had any canvas or trimmings or anything. He pawned everything. You daren't have left your box or your scissors or anything over night. He would have pawned the lot. He used to make up parcels, a good bit of good cloth on the outside and a bundle of rags and clippings stuffed inside the roll. Then he tied all that up in a nice piece of brown paper and string and away he went to Jimmy Lavery's. Lavery would only have torn a corner off the parcel. When he saw the cloth he might have said "The same again Johnny, a quid." He gave Johnny a pound and a pawn ticket and threw the parcel up on the rack. He never looked what was in it. One day Johnny hadn't even enough and he wrapped up wee lumps of turf inside the cloth in the parcel. Lavery didn't cop on for months. When Lavery opened the parcels he discovered that he had been had and he chased Johnny and told him never to darken his door again ...

I couldn't even get him to buy a stamp. I had to buy them myself. You needed ten to get back on the 'buroo.' I had to buy them myself. He would hardly mark them for me ... You worked ten weeks for nothing. Couldn't get money out of him.

In the nineteen-twenties a tailor would have charged about 25 shillings (£1.25) for making a suit. Some might have made one for fifteen. We had a big long gas heater to set the irons on and we pressed all the stuff on the floor. We had all shapes and sizes of irons, including "a goose." We had a big pad for laying on the floor. We used to talk about shrinking rather than pressing. A lot of the trousers were "bell mouthed." You had to take it to "the waterfall" to get it right.

The tailors called it whipping the cat"

THE BELLE OF THE PARISH

When Andy arrived, Peggy was the belle of the parish - rosy cheeked, auburn-haired, and well turned out. She used to set off to town in a pony-drawn phaeton, the only one in the district - and the cynosure of all eyes. Her parents had left her moderately well-heeled (very much so in comparison with her near neighbours) and she inherited a home that was a model of good taste and good housekeeping. "You could have licked meal off the floor" is how the old folk put it. Just after the death of the old folk, Peggy endowed a gable window in the parish church at something like £600 - big money around 1918. It was the principal window. All the rest cost only about a quarter of £600.

Her fortunes deteriorated rapidly. In the nineteen twenties, small farmers got a rough ride, and a lone woman like Peggy got the roughest of all. Andy hadn't a clue of course, and had to make matters worse, either he, or Peggy, or both, decided he had musical talent. He had a fairly pleasant singing voice, and he was sent to the top music teacher in Lurgan, a man called Smyth, to have his voice trained. Peggy also bought him a grand piano and a large HMV gramaphone. To practise his music he needed soft hands, hence heavy manual farm work was out. Lessons in singing and music were costly in terms of time and money, since he had to cycle five miles to town. One thing with another, he was more of a liability than an asset. He tried to emulate McCormick, but he never quite made the grade!

He wasn't entirely unskilled, which was perhaps unfortunate, for he soon embarked on a tool-buying spree. Each Saturday night he headed for Johnston's hardware store and eagerly snapped up the latest items in Joe McLaughlin's tool department. In fact Joe soon began to order anything unusual which travellers had to offer, knowing that Andy would take the bait. Soon Peggy's barn housed the best equipped workshop in the country. Andy never made anything with the tools, but it must be conceded that he did fix things, occasionally.

Every Saturday evening he made a scheduled run to Lurgan on his bike, with a wicker basket containing up to 24lbs of butter on the carrier. In town his regular customers queued up at the Mill Street corner shop awaiting his arrival. For years, he never let them down, not even when Peggy's herd of cows ceased to give milk! More about that later.

Peggy had had her eye on a near neighbour called Paddy Murray, a farmers' son who had emigrated to America. He came back in time to see his father, who was on the way out. When the old man died, there were complications over his will, and while these were being sorted out Paddy got work at a Belfast Shipyard.

In the pogrom of nineteen twenty, he narrowly escaped assassination there. A Protestant work-mate smuggled him out, brought him his coat and he got away. Many of the small number of Catholics in the workforce were kicked into the Lagan basin, and bombarded with rivets and pieces of iron until they drowned. Paddy never went back to Queen's Island, instead he resolved to leave Ireland for good, which he did in April 1921, leaving a disconsolate Peggy behind.

Whether or not Paddy's departure was a factor, or not, it is hard to say, but from then on Peggy began to go rapidly down hill. Trips to town became very rare, and the hens could be seen roosting on the phaeton, in later years. Possibly, she became depressed when the bills accumulated and income dried up. Anyhow self-neglect, and wretchedness got hold of her and, as she advanced in years, she became pitiful to behold as she struggled around the farmyard, striving to cope with stock-raising, attired in begrimed sacking, and manure-caked boots. She went nowhere, and no one, or very few, ever went to visit her. The house fell into disrepair; manure accumulated in mini-mountains outside every out-building; and all was dirt and misery. The grand piano fell apart with damp, and the parlour floor rotted beneath it. The kitchen-cum-living room eventually resembled a municipal dump, cluttered with sooty buckets, pots, butter boxes and thorn branches for firewood.

On the farm, starvation took its toll of livestock. Horses went down in the stable or in the grazing field with weakness, and neighbours had to rally round and use carts and ropes to hoist them to their feet. They usually survived a few such lifts, but no more. The vet was often on the scene, initially, but soon his services were dispensed with. Why he did not call the cruelty-to-animals people is a mystery; but possibly he had sympathy with the plight of impoverished farmers in those hungry years.

Meanwhile, Andy sailed on, regardless .... always looking well-fed and well-groomed. His weekly butter runs continued uninterrupted, as wonder grew in the parish as to where the butter was coming from. Some suspected he was buying in cheap margarine, but churning it in buttermilk. Anyhow his avid "town" customers ate away at Andy's popular country butter (sic), blissfully unaware of the conditions of the dairy from which it came. The country people just chortled "What they don't know, will do them no harm."

Eventually, Andy arived at our house in a panic, at dawn, one day with news that "auntie", as he called her, was dead. Those who went to his aid found only one bedroom habitable and the old lady dead in the only bed in the house. The kitchen was semi-habitable, but the rest of the house was down, or almost so. Spades had to be procured to remove two inches of clay from the tiled floors, and carts had to be brought in hurriedly to remove the heaps of manure, which cluttered the precincts of the dwelling. The belle of the parish had come to a sad end, leaving little but glar and misery for Andy to inherit.

He didn't delay long till he sold the lot, which was heavily mortgaged, taking with him back to Belfast a local teenage girl as a wife. He never did become a musician, or a singer, and neither had he become a farmer. He had, however, made an indelible mark on the history of the quiet rural area, to which he had come as a teenage orphan some 30 years earlier.

"Neglect and wretchedness got hold of her"

THE SECRET

Young Artie McGeown hid inside the stable door until the doctor left, but as soon as Doctor Minford got into his pony's trap and moved off, he pounced on his mother as she turned to go indoors.

"Can I go, Ma? Can I go now? Can I ...?"

He froze when his mother turned around, wiping tears from her face with the tail of her apron.

"What's wrong, Ma?", he shouted, "What are you crying about? Is Da very bad? Is he going to die ...?"

His mother put her arm around his shoulder; "Shush! It's all right son, it's just that I am vexed. Don't mind ME."

Re-assured, Artie started again, "Can I go, Ma? Can I go, Ma? I have the harness on and everything."

"Yes", his mother replied, "Yoke the horse and I will give you a hand with the bags. I'll have to check that they are all right. Mrs O'Neill is very particular. Get the money from her if you can. We could do with it."

In less that half-an-hour Arties was off down the rampart, perched on the topmost bag of turf on the cart. At 16, and not long left school, he felt on top of the world. It was the first time that he had been let out alone with the horse and cart. Only the 'squish, squish' of the horses hooves in the peaty soil and the rhythmic 'click of the trace chain on the hook of the hames, marking each stride of the horse, broke the stillness. Soon the grind of the iron-shod wheels and the ring of the horse's shoes on stone marked his exit onto the county road. Artie felt like cheering, but the sight of Ned Mullan's jaunting car coming along stopped him. Instead, he began whistling, "The Wearing of the Green."

As Mullan's fine trotting pony drew alongside, Ned waved his whip in salute, and his two female passengers 'kee hoed' and waved as well. Artie recognised them as the Yanks from Stevenson's and he kept hoping that more people would come along to see him, but he was disappointed. Then he began to feel guilty about being glad. Maybe his father was very bad? The doctor had spent a good while talking before he left. Maybe his mother wasn't telling him everything. He got down and walked a stretch, felt hungry, and got up again to look for the bread and milk his mother had put in between the sacks. The sauce bottle with it's plug of newsprint for a cork had leaked, and the milk was all gone. One bit of dry bread was all he ate - for he realised that he had a long journey ahead. Mrs O'Neill lived at Blayney's Hill away beyond "The Cash".

He was really hungry by the time he got there and when Mrs O'Neill met him like a bear with a sore head and started grousing about his father's not coming he felt like crying. "I want those turf stacked right," she grumbled, "What's the use of your father sending you?"

Meekly, Artie assured her that he would put the turf anywhere she wanted them ... Then he explained that the doctor had been to see his father and that he was in bed.

Mrs O'Neill softened immediately, "Come along, dear," she said, "and I'll show you where to put them."

When he had stacked the turf exactly as she wanted them, Artie went in for Mrs O'Neill, who immediately came out to check his work. She was well satisfied, and said so.

"Come in," she said, "you must be starving."

Artie didn't need to told twice. He slipped the nosebag on the horse and followed Mrs O'Neill indoors where she plied him with questions about his father, as she fed him on bread and milk with lashings of blackcurrant jam. Finally' she asked, "What about the money? Did your father say anything?"

"Ma said I was to get it if I could," Artie replied frankly. "She said Da mightn't be able to come for it for a good while and that she could be doing with it."

Mrs O'Neill immediately brought the money, wrapped it in brown paper and supervised Artie as he put it in an inside pocket, admonishing him not to lose it.

With his job completed and the money in his pocket, Artie felt big and happy and he snuggled down on a bag of hay in the empty cart. Once the horse was headed for home he needed no driver. Artie was nearly asleep when he heard shouts as he passed Greer's smithy. He looked up and saw big John Lennon hurrying towards him. He stopped the horse and Lennon looked puzzled when he laid his hand on the wing of the cart.

"Where's your father?", he demanded.

When Artie explained, big John said, "I have a very important message for Jimmy McAlinden. I wanted your father to give it to him. I don't think it would be safe with you".

Artie felt quite affronted, and immediately began to profess his reliability. Big John looked hard at him.

"If I were to give this to you (and he held up an envelope) and it got into the wrong hands, people could be put in gaol. I don't think I'll chance it."

Artie kept on making reassuring noises. "Honest to God John, I'll not let anybody but Jimmy see it; I'll give it to nobody else."

As Big John handed over the envelope he demanded, "Now what are you to do with this? Tell me."

"I am go give it to Jimmy McAlinden as soon as I can and let nobody else see it, or lay a hand on it."

"Right," Big John said, "Remember, you could get somebody arrested if you don't do exactly as I have told you."

Artie immediately felt great. He smelt conspiracy and he was delighted to be in on it. He felt really good.

Lennon went back towards Greer's and Artie drove off. When the horse reached Hunter's rampart it immediately turned off the road, unbidden. The noise of the cart wheels died. Artie looked back as he crossed the rampart, remembering what Dean Mooney had told him about ramparts - how the native Irish, driven out by the planters, had managed to get the tenancy of five-acre plots of bogland from the settlers and erected dwelling houses - first crude shelters made of sods, then mud-walled cabins, and how each had had a "right-away" down to the shore of Lough Neagh to draw water. They had eventually put on a hard-bottomed cart-track, to give access to the main road, and these ramparts, as they called them, had always been identified with the names of the men who had put them on. A man called Hunter had once lived where Artie's father lived now. Jimmy McAlinden lived beside him.

Artie spotted Jimmy fixing a turf stack in his haggard behind the house and he stopped the cart, and headed in his direction. As he walked close to Jimmy's door, Mrs McAlinden beckoned and he went to her. He had the note in his hand.

"Watch the Peeler," Mrs McAlinden whispered.

"What Peeler?" Artie queried. But just then Sergeant Beckett appeared around the gable of the house. His eye lit on the envelope immediately. "Is that for me?"

he queried. "Give it to me if you please."

"No," snapped Artie, "It's for him.", and he stuffed it up his jersey.

The Sergeant's face froze. "Oh!" he said, "For James? And who gave it to you?"
"I'm not telling you," Artie snarled.

"Aren't you now?" smirked the Sergeant. "Quite the big fella, aren't you! Just hand that envelope to me, if you please. now!"

"*I will not.*" Artie screamed as he dodged past him and ran over to Jimmy.

The Sergeant got there first however, and held out his hand.

"Give me that envelope young fella-me-lad." he insisted.

Jimmy intervened. "You had better do as the Sergeant tells you, Artie," he said.

Crestfallen, Artie handed over the envelope. The Sergeant opened it, read the note and beamed. "Ha! Just as I suspected," he cackled. "A band practice in the Crow Hall. Bring your own instrument," he rehearsed. "There's no Crow Hall. Bring your own instrument," he repeated. "There's no Crow Hall, for a start. And I never heard of James here being a musician. A Fenian drill, more likely. Tell me, more, young fella. Who gave you this? Some band practice! Artie dropped his head but gave no reply. The Sergeant's face darkened. "James, maybe you would like to tell me," he said, looking Jimmy straight in the eye.

"I know nothing about it," Jimmy replied blandly. "The note is not for me, and I know nothing about where it came from or anything else." The Sergeant realised that he was stone-walled, so he tackled Artie again.

"Young McGeown," he said, "I am giving you *one* more chance. Tell me where you got this and who it was for."

Artie remained silent and the Sergeant's temper boiled. "Oh! So you are going to act the big fellow," he thundered. "Bring that animal with you, till I talk to your father."

"You can't," Artie muttered. "He's in bed, sick." But he did as he had been bid, and led the horse home with Beckett alongside him.

As soon as his mother spotted the policeman she ran out shouting - "What's wrong, Sergeant? Has he had an accident? Is there anything wrong?"

"Oh! Calm yourself Missus!", the Sergeant replied. "I just want this young man to tell me where he was and who he saw, but he is being awkward."

"What is it you want to know?" Mrs McGeown demanded, "He was at O'Neill's with a load of turf. Didn't he tell you that? There's no secret about it!"

"Ah!" the Sergeant explained. "That's not the mystery. He brought a letter to James McAlinden and he won't say where he got it."

"Artie!" Mrs McGeown gasped, "Will you tell the Sergeant what he wants to know and let us have no more nonsense. As if I haven't enough worry about your father. What's this all about?"

Artie stayed silent. Then as his mother seized him by the shoulders and shook him, "I'm not telling. Leave me alone, Ma, will you. I'm not telling." he shouted.

His mother stood speechless, with a dazed look on her face.

"Sergeant," she said "I just don't understand what's going on between you two. You have rubbed him the wrong way. Why can't you just be easy with him? His father will be out of his sick bed with this narration, if we are not careful. Leave off, and I'll talk to him, when he gets the horse loosed out."

At this stage Artie's father appeared at the doorway of his house, clad only in a shirt. Mrs McGeown dashed over to get him back to bed, and the Sergeant promptly seized Artie by the arm, gave him a shake and hissed -

"You are not in trouble yet - but you could be. Get that animal into the stable. I haven't finished with you yet. Not by a long chalk. Don't try your smart-alex tricks with me, or you'll rue it."

Artie did as he was ordered and put the cart in it's place, unyoked the horse and put him in the stable. As he removed the harness his mother returned, in a frenzied state. She immediately gave Artie a tongue-thrashing about unsetting his sick father, and herself as well, but she might as well have been talking to the wall. Artie had got his back up and he was not prepared to listen to anyone. He just kept repeating, stubbornly,

"Leave me alone. Leave me alone. Why can't you all just leave me alone."

The Sergeant chimed in with words of advice but he got nowhere. Then he decided he would have to assert his authority.

"I'm sorry Missus," he said, "but if this young fellow is not going to talk here, I'll have to take him to the barracks."

Mrs McGeown blanched and grasped the jamb of the door to steady herself. Artie's face paled too, but his teeth remained clinched. He tried to run out, but the Sergeant caught him and barked,

"Now don't you try any tricks. You wouldn't like me to snap these bracelets on you, would you?" and he pointed to the handcuffs on his belt.

At this Mrs McGeown got hysterical, but the Sergeant calmed her down.

"I'm just taking him in to answer a few questions. No need to worry. The sooner he tells me all about the note the sooner he'll be home again. He's just acting the big fellow. When he has been in the barracks half-an-hour, he'll change his tune. Right, young fellow," he said, "come with me" and he marched Artie off towards McAlinden's were he had his bicycle. Then he headed for Trasna cross-roads with a firm grip of Artie. Seeing a squad of "B" Specials sitting on the ditch there, Artie's heart sank. He recognised his immediate neighbour, Sam Martin, as one of them and he knew that he was the sub-district commandant. The Sergeant spoke to Martin, then got on his bicycle and went off. Martin immediately stepped over to Artie and said, What kind of an eejit are you, young McGeown. The Sergeant has gone for a Crossley tender to take you in. Why couldn't you answer his questions and not get yourself into trouble? Covering up for Lennon who doesn't care a damn about you"

He continued bully ragging Artie on and off until the Crossley tender arrived. Artie's heart sank still further when he saw the militia seated back to back on the tail of it with rifles between their knees. As the driver slowed down to turn, two "B men" jumped off and grabbed Artie. He was dumped aboard like a sack of spuds and the old banger roared off in a haze of smoke with the lad sandwiched between two burly 'specials'.

The Crossley made more noise than speed as it back-fired and chugged along. Before it reached the barracks it stopped completely and the driver jumped down and raised the bonnet.

"Youse may walk the rest," he announced. "The mag. has packed up."

As the Specials scrambled down, one of them snapped handcuffs on Artie and he was marched off to the barracks like a criminal. He was questioned for hours but still refused to talk and next day he found himself in a cell at Crumlin Road Gaol in Belfast. Before the day was out he was hauled before a special court and remanded in custody under the Special Powers Act.

— — — — — — — —

Now, nearly 70 years later, Artie was re-living it all. As a feeble old man without chick or child he had just got a death sentence from his doctor. He had known before he had gone to hear the results of the tests. The doctor in the hospital had as good as told him that he had cancer.

All his life he had revelled in a feeling of grim satisfaction that, since the day he had been arrested, he had never looked at the side of the road where Martin was, although they had farmed within a mile of each other. The memory of the month in gaol still rankled.

What Father Mattie had said last week, when they had discussed it, was also still niggling him. "Artie," he had said, "When you say your prayers just think ... as we forgive those who trespass against us."

Artie knew that Sam Martin, now in his nineties, was also 'a-waiting-on', and that they were going to "go home" together. He decided to take the bull by the horns, and headed down the road to his good neighbour Henry Murray's house. When he asked him if he would run him over to Martin's. Henry opened his mouth to say something - then froze. "All right Artie," he said, "if that's what you want, come on."

Artie got into the car and as soon as they got to Martin's he stepped out in silence and went to the door. Young Mrs Martin opened it, and if she was surprised, she didn't show it. Instead, she greeted him warmly and led him into a downstairs bedroom where her father-in-law lay.

Artie was visibly shaken as he beheld the tiny doll-like figure, with cherub features, and bright black eyes, propped up in the bed. Surely this was not the burly six-footer whom he had contended with 70 years ago?

"How are you, Frank?" he queried. "I don't think we have met since the Moy Fair. Do you mind that wee bay mare that you helped me to buy? Boy, she grew into a good one."

Artie realised with a shock that the old man had taken him for his long-dead father. He was about to try to put him right, but before he could speak the old man went on.

"What about that young fellow of yours, young Artie - the one who got himself into trouble trying to save the skin of that good-for-nothing, Lennon. I always liked that lad, Frank. He had spunk, and, if he had ever given chance I would have told him. What about getting Ned Mullan to run us to the Moy on Thursday. Bring the young fellow with you and we'll teach him how to judge a horse."

With tears blinding him, Artie turned to Mrs Martin, only to find her wearing a broad smile. The realisation came that she had not even been born when he had last met her father-in-law. "He's funny, isn't he?" she remarked, "Living in the past all the time."

Artie decided to humour Sam. "Right Sam" he said, "I'll get Ned and we will make a day of it. See you on Thursday morning."

"How did you get on?" Harry queried. "Oh! The very best. The very best."

57

"He kept hoping more people would see him"

THE THORN TREE

"Heavens, Charlie! Why don't you take the billhook to them things and not be jagging the hands off yourself?"

Charlie Breen, who had been methodically tying back the branches of a big thorn tree, with bits of grass rope, paused, looked around, and grinned. "Ach, Sammy," he drawled, "you like to have your wee joke. Have you got a match?"

Sammy Johnston had brought his bicycle to a standstill and planted one foot on the ditch. Silently, he handed a box of matches to Charlie. The latter lit his pipe, absent-mindedly pocketed the matches, took a couple of deep draws, and continued.

"The last man who laid a hook on those was my grandfather. It fell out of his hand and they discovered he had got a stroke. He was carried home and he never rose from his bed."

"Holy Heavens, Charlie! Don't tell me you believe stuff like that! It's all a lot of baloney," mocked Sammy.

Charlie ignored the taunt, and resumed tying up the twigs. Meanwhile Sammy was eyeing the trees speclatively. With a prolonged coal strike going on, there were few like them still standing in the hedgerows in 1926. Eventually, he quipped.

"Now Charlie! Would you like to give me back my matches, you aul chancer?"

Sheepishly, Charlie fished the box from his pocket and apologised. Sammy said, "Cherrio," and pedalled off. Then having cleared the way for the horses to turn at the end of the furrows, Charlie picked up the reins and resumed ploughing operations.

Johnston was a Belfast man who had moved out to the country during the depression. He had lost his job in the shipyard and times were hard. Most of the locals had managed to stockpile some fuel, but he hadn't been so lucky. He had no money.

As the Winter wore on, he and his wife and children ranged far and wide gathering sticks, but landowners were getting a bit resentful and the quest more hopeless. One night in January he made up his mind and picked up his bicycle lamp. As soon as he did so his schoolboy son, Jimmy, became inquistive. "Are you going to the river, Da?" he queried.

"No! I'm not going to any - so and so - river" his father growled.

"Where are you going? Can I come with you? Can I, Da?" he persisted.

"No! You can't. It's bedtime. Get to your bed", Sammy growled.

Jimmy started to whimper.

"I have no school tomorrow, Da. Why can I not go with you ------ Can I, Da, ... Please ...."

Sammy relented. It had struck him that he would need someone to hold the lamp.

"All right," he muttered crossly. "Get your wellies and your coat. And no chat. We are going quietly."

Jimmy was out after him before he had laid hands on the saw and the hatchet from the shed. He threw the lad a coil of rope, gave him the saw and said. "Come on. Hurry!"

Jimmy was terrified of the dark, having been city bred.

"Light the lamp, Da," he said "I'm afraid."

"Afraid or no afraid, we are lighting no damned lamp," his father grunted. "Here hang on to me." Timidly, and expecting a demon to pounce from every bush, Jimmy followed, clutching his father's coat.

Up the lane to the stile, over into Ellis' sand field, and across towards Ashvale they went. Sammy knew every hole in the hedges, which he had scoured for firewood. Eventually, they emerged on to the Kilmore Road, and a short distance along stopped at Breen's thorn tree. Sammy showed Jimmy how to conceal the bicycle lamp under his coat, then he lit it and started to work with the saw on the larger tree. The saw made an errie noise in the still dark night, and when a terrified wood pigeon fled noisely from above, Jimmy yelled in terror and dropped the lamp. Sammy jabbed him with his knee, swore at him and retrieved it.

"Another squeak out of you and I'll send you home," he threatened.

The mere threat terrified the boy and he clung tightly to his father's legs. Debris and withered leaves began to shower down as his father sawed away. Then the whole bush started to quiver like an aspen. At first, Sammy thought it was the vibration, but when the timber closed on the saw he was forced to stop. Still the quivering continued as he reached for the hatchet, and he noticed that the wind had risen. This puzzled him for the night had been frosty and still. As Jimmy clung closer to him, he began to feel a bit jumpy himself. He shrugged off his unease, cleared the saw, and went on cutting. Fear impelled him to attack the tree with fierce strokes and be done with it. As he did so, there was a loud crack and the trunk splintered. He barely had time to shove Jimmy out of danger, when he went down. He never knew what hit him.

As he lay stunned, buried by the fallen tree, Jimmy yelled in terror.

"Da! Da! Are you all right, da? Da speak to me."

There was no answer, and as the lad flashed the light on his father's head he saw blood. Hysterically, he called to his father, again and again, then he panicked. He could see a light in Breen's window and he sped towards it, screaming like a wounded hare and dropping the lamp in his headlong flight. Reaching Breen's he grasped the latch on the door and virtually swung on it as he hurled himself around the jamb wall into the kitchen.

Charlie and his brother, Joe, leaped from their seats on either side of the hearth, shouting in unison.

"What ails you Jimmy. What's wrong?"

"It's my da", Jimmy screamed. "Come quick, m'da is dead!"

Charlie seized the boy by the shoulders as he continued to blubber hysterically and eventually he got the gist of the story.

"He's under the fairy thorn. He was cutting it down and it fell on him. He's bleeding and he can't speak. Come quick."

The Breens immediately rushed outside. Charlie gabbed a plank from the barn, and Joe brought a hurricane lamp. Jimmy clung to Joe's hand and wouldn't let go, as they ran towards the tree.

When they got there the men prised it aside and examined Sammy. He was semi-conscious and babbling about lights and about "them," having tied his feet. Gently, they lifted him up and as they did so a torrent of foul language flowed from him.

"Take that bloody spear out of my hand," he yelled. Then he came round. Charlie looked him over and observing a particularly wicked thorn embedded in the back of Sammy's hand, he deftly removed it with his teeth.

"That's as sharp as any spear, Sammy," he wryly remarked.

Sammy was able to walk to Breen's with help, and when they got him there they had a look at his head. It turned out that his wound was superficial, but bloody, so they tied it up for him and made him a cup of tea.

While he supped it, Charlie chided him, "You must have been very ill off for firewood, when you couldn't leave the fairy thorn alone." "Indeed, I am Charlie," Sammy confessed. We haven't a stick to boil the kettle and the wee lassie seems to be taking fever. The wife is frantic. I don't know what I am going to do. I suppose I might as well take the thorn now when I have cut it."

"No! No! Sammy," the brothers shouted at him in unison. Then Charlie continued, "You will just leave that thorn alone. You have had enough bad luck. Go home and bring over the barrow and we will give you some firewood to keep you going

Sammy did as he was bidden and he was back before bedtime for the load of wood.

Next day the doctor was with the sick child. When he had gone, Charlie, and Joe hurried over to learn that he had diagnosed pleurisy, with a threat of pneumonia and ordered that she should be kept warm. As the old boys left, they noticed the half-empty barrow, but neither passed any remark, and it was only after tea that they got round to discussing how to get the fallen tree out of the horses' way. Their problem was quickly solved when their married sister burst in through the door in a flaming temper.

"What's this about you not letting Sammy Johnston have the aul thorn bush?" she demanded. "Are you going to sit there and let their wee girl die? I have told Sammy to come and get the horse and cart and fetch the thing. You had better give him a hand."

Meekly, her two brothers headed for the stable.

"... buried by the fallen tree"

DICK THE BUTCHER

The ferocity of Carlo's growl as he cleared the haggard ditch in a frenzied leap was a sure sign that he had scented blood. As Dick-the-butcher approached across the Sand Field and the gap between them narrowed, it was hard to judge which was becoming the more incensed, the dog or the pig butcher.

"Dammit sowl, call up that dog. Call him up quick!" Dick yelled. "D'ye hear me? Call that bloody dog home Will-um! he guldered.

He always pronounced "William" as "Will-um."

As Dad followed the dog at a jog trot and eventually subdued him, he shouted back to me.

"Tell Bill that Dick's here."

Dick's tune changed as soon as the dog turned tail.

"Is the water boiling, Willum? I'm away behind time. I've a day's work to do before dark."

He was nearly an hour late and the farm boiler had gone off the boil. Bill hastily stuffed some old timber saturated with paraffin oil, into the fire box, when I yelled at him - "Dick's here, Bill, and he's as crabbit as a weasel."

Soon the wailing of pigs told us that Dick was in the pig-sty roping his first victim. Carlo took off again and confronted Dick as he emerged with his victim.

"Call up that bloody mongrel, Willum, will ye!" he thundered. Actually it was Dick who was bloody, the stink of gore and the clank of steels and knives strung round his belt was enough to excite any dog.

I ran across the haggard to see Dick in action and as soon as I was within earshot, Dad whispered.

"Has Bill the water boiling?"

I shook my head and Dad immediately distracted Dick by pointing to a beam which he had erected on the front of the hayshed for extra carcases. Dick knew that there were six pigs to be killed and that there was only space for four on the lintel above the high door to the barn. With the introduction of dry-feeders, pig production had doubled and Dick was being hard pressed to cope.

"Do you think it will do?" Dad queried.

Dick had a rope fastened to the two hind legs of a porker and he had difficulty in standing still long enough to inspect the beam.

"Why, Hell, Willum it wud howl a ton," he guldered, as the porker nearly tossed him. He gave it a thump with the lath that he had in his hand and virtually trailed the doomed animal to the place of slaughter. Deftly, Dad seized the rope and threw the animal on its back on the threshold to the barn as Dick drew his razor-sharp knife from its scabbard, grabbed one of the animal's forelegs, and made the kill.

The animal barely had time to squeal when its life blood flooded the floor and the noise died to a whimper. Dick never missed the heart. We made a point of checking the location of the incision when the heart was extracted for market.

We also eagerly seized the pig's bladder which we inflated with a bicycle pump and used as a football.

The moment the squeals had died to a whimper, and whilst the carcase was still quivering, Dick put away his rapier-type knife, extracted a broad blade one from his belt, and reached for the kettle of boiling water with his left hand. The kettle *had* to be within reach, and the water piping hot. Dad looked anxiously at Bill as he laid down the kettle but he stayed quiet till Dick poured on the stream and began scraping. When he didn't complain but pressed on, all of us breathed easily again. The crisis had passed. Nothing infuriated Dick like delay in providing hot water, and the whole country knew it. He really went berserk and held his customers to ransom over the issue, for he was a perfectionist and he expected perfection from all his attendants - even more than perfection when he was pushed for time. Twenty minutes to rope, slay, and dress the carcase - three to the hour - and the end-product pristine, was his target, and Heaven help anyone within reach of his tongue who bungled. As a pig butcher, he reigned supreme and held a monopoly on his patch, which was close to Lough Neagh's banks.

True to form, he had to fifth carcase ready to hang in little over an hour and a half later. The first four had been strung up over the threshold of the barn door but the fifth had to go on the newly-erected beam. All went well until the sixth, and last, was ready and Dad and Dick heaved on the rope to hoist the carcase aloft, heels up. There was a loud crack and the sound of splintering timber as two carcases slid on to the muddy haggard!

Dick just opened his mouth and stood aghast. The tongue-thrashing which Dad expected never came. Instead the butcher immediately hauled one carcase on to clean ground, and shouted.

"Where's Bill! Get me more water quick!"

No time was lost in getting him more water and in a few minutes he had the carcase in pristine condition again.

"Here, Willum," he shouted, "Grab that rope and come on to that ash tree over there. We'll soon have the two of them hung up again."

The big increase in pig farming which took place in the nineteen-twenties ought to have been a boon and a blessing to Dick, but indirectly it led to his undoing.

As a crotchety old man with a captive clientele of small farmers who had no one else to turn to when they had one pig, or two, ready for the pork market he had had difficulty in stomaching his primitive methods, but they were afraid to object.

More pigs to kill took him out into deeper waters with a clientele who had more clout, and who were less reticent in their criticism. A young whippersnapper set up in opposition, which did not help although dire warnings were circulated about the risk of an amateur "shoulder-sticking" a pig and having the carcase downgraded by the buyer.

The authorities moved in to enforce the use of humane-killers and Dick lost confidence. He never used the weapon personally, but always looked to the farmer to actually fire the shot. Soon he packed up altogether with advancing age and "new fangled things" bothering him.

"The kettle had to be within reach"

ANNABELLA

With nothing else to do in the shop, Mrs O'Neill had time to eye her employer, Charlie Mullen, as he reversed out of the garage and waited for Bertie Mossey to arrive. He hadn't long to wait. Bertie drove up, parked his old banger, and off they went. She knew that they were heading for a point-to-point meeting.

Charlie's brother, Johnny, had died recently, and Mrs O'Neill was feeling low. She had been with Mullens for 60 years, as housekeeper/shop assistant and she would have liked to have seen Charlie married but he seemed to have no interest. His mother Monica was to blame for that. She had lived until he was in his fifties and neither Johnny nor Charlie would ever have dared to bring in another women in her day.

She hated to see Charlie knocking around with Mossey, for she knew he was a lazy sponger. She also knew that he would always let Charlie pick up the bills. Not long back, he had wormed his way round old Miss McCormick the school-mistress and as soon as he had got her to marry him he had started gadding about again, like a single man. Everyone knew it had been her money he had been after.

She decided to go into the house for a cup of tea knowing that Rose, who did the housework, would have the kettle boiling. As she stepped outside she glanced up at the sign over the shop door. "Monica Mullan & Sons". It had read "James Mullan" when she had arrived, - "James Mullan - Auctioneer and General Merchant." The older folk though Monica might have left the old name be when James died but she liked to let people see who was boss. Now, with Johnny gone, Charlie was a very rich man - the last of his line and with neither chick nor child.

Mullan's residence, Kilnacross House, next door to the shop was the hub of the village of the same name, and because of his autioneering business Charlie was widely known. In the evenings when he was at home the place never slackened.

All the lame dogs came to Charlie, and half the parish owed him money, but he kept no records and charged no interest. He was a religious man, and took his duty of helping the poor seriously, but no one could size up a chancer better than he.

Charlie was in no hurry to find a wife, or a shop manager. Mrs O'Neill had been a second mother to him and he was happy enough so long as she carried on. That wasn't as long as he had expected. One January day she slipped and broke her femur. While she was laid up in hospital he and Bertie had had to take over the shop. He didn't like being behind the counter, and neither did Bertie.

Always "the fixer" Bertie started to look around, without prompting. One Wednesday he arrived with a fine looking red-head, whom he introduced as Annabella Wilson. He explained that she was tired travelling to the city. Charlie knew Annabella's family and he was aware that she had a good job in Woolworth's. With trade in the shop at a low level, he saw no prospects of affording Annabella, and he said so. She surprised him by revealing that she wasn't looking for anything like Woolworth's salary. What she wanted was a place nearer home and shorter hours. Travelling to the city was at least a ten-hour day. After some discussion they settled for a modest wage and a built-in commission on sales. Annabella accepted, as she liked a challenge. As well, she had weighed up other possibilities and they looked attractive.

With Mrs O'Neill in hospital, Charlie was glad to have congenial company. Annabella had a good way with people and very soon business began to pick up. Charlie gave her almost a free hand but he popped in once a day, at least, and he began to feel less inclination to leave home. Bertie didn't quite know what to make of him when he started singing Annabella's praises. He wanted to keep up the momentum of race-going, but on the other hand nothing would have pleased him better than for his friend, Annabella, to get round Charlie.

Annabella was a mature lady and too close to forty for her own liking and in common with other local spinsters she had long had her eye on Charlie, in spite of his age and poor physical condition. The closer she got to him as the days went by the more attracted she became for he was one of nature's gentlemen - kindly, good-humoured and generous. She recognised before long that he had been used to mothering and she was very happy to treat him like an overgrown schoolboy.

Charlie, on his part, had no experience of femine charms. He found Annabella physically attractive, and the lady used perfume and plunging necklines to the best advantage, but she carefully avoided physical contact, lest she would scare him off, for she saw that he was painfully shy. The nearest contacts she could engineer were frequent queries about invoices etc., requiring them to put their heads together to analyse entries. Then she could feel the electricity flowing, and very cautiously she prolonged the *tete-a-tete*. One day, for devilment, when she was perched on the house-steps stocking a shelf, with Charlie handing tins up to her, she faked a loss of balance. While still a couple of feet from the ground she caused the steps to topple and managed to fall, on Charlie's broad shoulders. His wide grin and playful disentaglement thrilled her, but above all his obvious concern about her safety thrilled her more. As they sorted themselves out she was sorely tempted to keep her arms round him and plant her lips on his, but thought better of it. Charlie, unbeknownst to her, was tempted too but his innate shyness took over. Annabella was a women, but worse still she was an employee and, therefore, untouchable as far as he was concerned. Never the twain could meet.

Annabella saw the episode as an encouragement, but, with astute femine instinct, she realised that she still had a long way to go. Still, she had no opposition and she had him on her own ground she thought - and decided to play it cool and gently lead him on. Mrs O'Neill who had an eye on the two of them, now that she was mobile again and very close, didn't like what she saw. She decided that, "her ladyship" as she termed Annabella, wouldn't wrap Charlie round her finger, if she could stop her. She diplomatically gave him hints to watch Annabella, any time opportunity presented itself, but she didn't overdo it. She relied on Charlie's gumption to keep Annabella in her place.

Charlie soon had more to think about than Annabella, when he got a huge income-tax bill in the Spring. His tax man had got bolshie. Charlie's accountant understood his client's preference for dealing in cash and dispensing with records, but the tax man was more suspicious and he had issued a shattering demand, based on estimates. Charlie and his accountant had either to provide chapter and verse or pay up.

Bertie was consulted - of course - still "The fixer" - he immediately brought Charlie along to meet his (Bertie's) cousin Annie Armstrong, who was fairly high up in a tax office (not the one dealing with Charlie's business.) Annie succeeded in setting up meetings with Mullan's tax inspector and eventually, after prolonged negotiations, the inspector accepted that Charlie had foolishly given out a lot of interest-free loans, which he was unlikely ever to recover, since he had no records. The demand was modified, and Charlie got off with a much reduced tax bill.

Naturally, he felt much indebted to Annie, and hinted at rewading her, but Bertie quickly convinced him that it would be an affront to offer any consideration. Charlie remained unhappy, however, and kept nagging. In the end, Bertie said "Why not ask her to join us in a day out at the Curragh and bring a friend?" Annie accepted the invitation and the foursome had a grand day out, finishing off at the Gresham Hotel in Dublin. Annie was a teetotaller, as was Charlie, but her pal was ready and willing to join Bertie in knocking back the liquor. As a result the foursome became two twosomes. On the way home, while the inevitable bantering was at its height, Bertie quickly suggested a repeat - this time at Galway races. Charlie took careful stock of Annie's reaction and he was delighted when she said, "Yes." In the mood which the other lady was in with Bertie, it was obvious that she was rearing to go.

Since Bertie was a married man his "fancy woman" as the locals soon termed her, found her name being dragged in the mud by the gossips of Kilnacross. That soon finished the outings to the races.

Charlie was vexed, for he and Annie had got on well but he just had to thole. Annabella had, of course, heard all about "the woman from the income tax office" and the atmosphere in the shop had become frigid. Mrs O'Neill, ever watchful, was delighted, when she saw that "her ladyship", as she called Annabella, was being thwarted.

Six months passed before Charlie encountered Annie again. Then they met outside the Linenhall Library in Belfast one day by chance. Annie greeted Charlie very warmly, and as soon as he laid eyes on her he realised how much he had been longing to see her again. They discussed previous outings and Charlie discovered that Annie had really enjoyed them. This encouraged him to invite her out for a meal, which she accepted immediately. Things moved very fast after that. Charlie deliberately said nothing to Bertie, but soon he was seeing Annie regularly, and getting very close. In three months time, at Christmas, he popped the question, and Annie said "Yes."

In the summer Charlie brought Annie home as his bride, and a right noisy reception the village gave them. Annie immediately encountered sullen hostitity from Annabella but she ignored it. As mistress and with time on her hands, she soon began to review the potential of the shop, which was doing very little trade. This she soon discovered, was because they did not stay open late, or on Wednesday afternoons. To get to know the regulars as soon as possible she moved in behind the counter, when she was free. She could sense sparks flying from Annabella when she began to serve the occasional customer, but worse was to come. Soon she found that no matter how hard she tried, she could never locate items on the shelves. Annabella was systematically re-arranging stock at frequent intervals to frustrate her. As well the cunning lady stopped putting prices on the more commonly-asked-for items. She knew them. Annie did not. This forced

Annie to ask Annabella constantly. Annabella was sweetness personified in the presence of customers as she assisted "the Mistress" to find things and to discover the price - making Annie look a right imbecile.

Annie knew she was being deliberately provoked but she was determined to out-smart the lady and bided her time. When the Christmas stock came in, she personally priced it and made Annabella help her, but lay-out was still a problem. Annabella claimed that frequent re-arrangements were necessary, because of lack of space, but their real purpose was clear.

When they closed for the Christmas holidays, Annie decided to put things where *she* wanted them and to put a price tag on everything. Charlie was peeved, but she refused to desist. He wanted to go off to Dublin and live it up, but Annie would have none of that till the job was completed. It took the whole of the holidays to complete and they had to burn the midnight oil, but before they re-opened all was shipshape.

Annabella's face was a picture as she viewed the new lay-out when she resumed after Christmas, and when Charlie invited her to approve she showed her venom.

"Nobody could find anything here," she grumped. Charlie, in an uncharacteristic show of authority, rebuked her. She was so surprised that she just opened her mouth..... No words came..... Instead, she stomped into the store and began moving stock. Then Annie announced in ringing tones; "Annabella, everything is to be left where I have arranged it and priced from now on - if you please. The boss and I have sweated over it for days and I don't want anything disturbed." Annabella made no answer, so she added - "From 1st January, we will stay open till 8.30 every evening, including Wednesdays but I won't ask you to work any longer hours," Annabella gave her a dirty look.

Fate took a hand early in the New Year. Annie's brother, Dan, who had a pub in Belfast city centre, died suddenly, and his only son, Pat, who had married into a West of Ireland family inherited the business. Pat had to move in temporarily with the Mullans and spend a lot of time in the pub. He was up and down to Belfast every day and one evening he came home in a bit of a panic as a barman had been bereaved. He wanted Annie to help out next day, but she demurred. Annabella, who had overheard, immediately volunteered. A spell in a Belfast bar appealed to her - so did the prospect of travelling up and down with Pat, for she fancied him.

She was quite a hit with customers in the bar - goodlooking, saucy and sociable. Pat found her very useful and he kept calling on her more and more frequently. Annie was happy to have her out of the shop and let Pat have her. It didn't dawn on her that Pat, as a young man separated from his wife from one week-end to another, was very vulnerable to a schemer like Annabella. Eventually she and Charlie let Pat take Annabella on permanently as a barmaid.

She still travelled home with Pat late at night and Mrs. O'Neill was the first to sound dire warning to the Mullans. Annie spoke to Pat and admonished him to be careful to keep Annabella in her place, but he just laughed, and assured her that he was well able to look after himself. Sometimes, they were very late home. Seemingly, Annabella insisted on washing up after the bar closed. "She hadn't been too keen on washing up here," Mrs. O'Neill caustically commented, and went as far as to say:

"Annie, will you, for heaven's sake, tell Pat that that woman is getting him a bad name."

When Charlie and Annie continued to sound warnings, Pat put an end to the late washing-up sessions, but otherwise, things remained the same.

After a couple of months, he got a hell of a shock when he discovered that Annabella was pregnant. Fingers were pointed at him immediately and, cunningly, Annabella said nothing to stop the gossip. Annie immediately suspected that Annabella was out to blacken Pat, in order to get her own back. She and Charlie cross-examined Pat about Annabella's letting people blame *him*. Pat quickly convinced them that nothing improper had ever occurred between Annabella and himself. The problem now was how to stop the gossip.

The travelling together had to stop. Pat thought up a domestic crisis involving his family and openly discussed his wife's inability to cope with his staff. Then he took soundings of his head barman about taking over as manager. The man leapt at the offer and soon Annabella was faced with the problem of commuting by bus. Pat had had to return home. She also found herself with a new employer.

She stuck it out for a while until she had to go on maternity leave and stay at home. When the child arrived and she made her first appearance in Kilnacross, with a very impressive baby carriage, she was overwhelmed by well wishers. The stampede to get a peep into that pram by the "nosey parkers" was wild. Some of them on the verge of incontinence. Who was it like?

All they saw was a wee red head the image of his "Ma" and Annabella's well beringed left hand. Those who had the temerity to comment got only an enigmatic smile and the sly comment "The two go together, you know."

It was only later when Pat's bar manager took his place at the baptismal font that the secret was out.

"She faked a loss of balance"

INISFREE

As Larry Phillips went to his station on the fourth floor landing to marshal the confluence of his colleagues flowing rapidly down the wide stone staricase of the multi-storied ofice building, his mood was one of depression. Every other day they had been out recently. This was the second bomb alert inside 48 hours, and there was no way of knowing whether or not it was another false alarm. The building had already been badly damaged on two occasions, but fortunately it had been empty, and there had been no casualties. Still! As usual, the bombers had been vague in their warning ... "a major government office near the city hall" could mean any one of half a dozen or more.

Although he had had long service, Larry was able to identify only a small number of the faces which passed him on their way down. As they tripped from one step to another at a steady pace, he only had to motion with his hands to maintain the momentum. There was no panic. No one involved had so far been caught in a blast and they regarded the alert as just another nuisance.

Usually Brian Faulkner and his Private Office staff would have been first down, but Ted Heath had changed the ball game. The Stormont Minister had been deposed and his successor from the Northern Ireland Office was absent, attending Parliament at Westminster. The Permanent Secretary was leading the procession out today. How does "Old Man River" go? ! he mused. "Men may come and men may go but I go on forever?" Permanent Secretaries and Ministers were a bit like that, he thought, but at least promotion prospects had improved with the take-over. Larry had been thinking a good deal about that lately but for him it had come too late and early retirement had begun to appeal to him.

After all these years, what was he except an extension number to the telephonists, "the big man in room 438" to the Messengers, and a voice on the 'phone, or a signature on a piece of paper to the man-in-the-street. Surveying the moving throng on the staircase, he gave a wry smile as the tag "faceless bureaucrats" sprang to his mind. Faceless bureaucrats tangled up in the rat race? .... a sinking ship? With an effort he put aside these unworthy musings. At least, he still had an identity on his native heath, he thought. Commuting so far each day had certainly become tedious, with bomb alerts on the trains, and workers' strikes, but it was worth it to get out of "bomb-alley" in the evenings. He knew that his wife was anything but happy. She certainly would be relieved if he should decide to call it a day.

What was it F.C. Moore had said the day he had been inducted into the service over 40 years ago?

"If the Northern Ireland government should happen to be abolished, your job will still be safe. It is permanent and pensionable and whatever government takes over will provide continuity of service."

He had never imagined he would need that guarantee but, lately, with all sorts of wild rumours circulating about possible U.D.I. and now the suspension of "Stormont" he found it reassuring. The early retirement-packet had begun to look very attractive, but, first, he needed time to work it all out in some quiet retreat.

As the evacuation continued in an orderly manner, the staff were marshalled to the side of the car park furtherest from the building, the babble of their voices loud in the unnatural stillness of traffic-free Victoria Square. Some Senior Officers gathered a few of their assistants together in impromptu mini-conferences, but mostly the rank and file were content to indulge in light-hearted chat.

The hub-bub was instantly switched off and some subdued shrieks went up when the not-unexpected bang took place. This one sounded more intense and more menacing than ever, and the frenzied flights of starlings overhead showed that the explosion had been close by.

The rumble of falling masonry and the jingle of shattering glass had barely died down when it seemed as if all hell had been let loose. First the wail of one siren, then another, and another and still another, marked the swift turn-out of all the fire appliances from Chichester Street Station. As they sped around the law courts and down May Street the notes of their sirens tangled, competed, and mingled in an ear-splitting cacophony.

The assembled officials had no difficulty in plotting the course of the fire brigade and when news was radioed to the Marshals that it was Fountain House which had been hit, no one was surprised. As they filtered back to the lifts inside the building, and returned to their offices, a subdued silence reigned. They all knew that it might just as easily have been their office, and the thought uppermost in most minds was "Maybe we will be next."

Larry Phillips shared the general air of gloom. Where was all this going to end? Totally unable to come to terms with the situation he resolved to take a break, outside Northern Ireland. He had plenty of leave due to him and on this pleasant day (in terms of weather) the familiar oft-quoted words of the poet Yeats which he loved so well, came to mind.

"I'll arise and go now .... and go to Inisfree." He picked up his leave chart, filled it up and strode down the corridor to his Senior Officer's room. He found it empty so he deposited the chart in the "IN" tray and went on his way, having already discussed his plans and got provisional clearance.

By next forenoon, he was over 100 miles from Belfast - on the winding banks of Erne, with Rosnowlagh beach as his destination. A wayside Monastery looked enticing, and he decided to pay a visit. Relaxing on a bench, while the family explored the grounds, Ketelbey's famour piece of music "In a Monastery Garden" immediately came to life. In this idyllic spot, with the honey bees loud in the herbaceous border at this feet, and a cheerful little robin singing on a bush, its scarlet breast gleaming in the sunshine, the contrast with the mayhem that he had left in Belfast was so stark that tears welled in his eyes.

Gloomily, he reflected, on what his fellow countrymen were doing to their native land .....

..... His reverie was disrupted by the jarring note of a jubilant hen cackling stridently in a tiny farmyard on an eminence beyond the river. Then the Angelus bell sounded, and in a moment he felt himself transported back through the years, to his childhood days in the farm haggard and the many idle hours which he had spent perched on a shaft of a farm cart in the hayshed, watching the activities of the barnyard fowl as they scratched and clucked in the litter. He recalled how the little marley hen which had been laying away, had proudly strutted home one day with her flock of fluffy chicks in tow. His mother had missed her, and tried to stalk her, in vain. How excited he had been when he raced indoors to announce that the marley hen was back, with wee chickens .....

Could he recapture those days he wondered? He knew he couldn't - not completely, but at least he could find relative peace once more. "That's it" he resolved. "I will pack it in, and go back to the country. I might even raise a few pheasants, as well as hens". With that, he went in search of the family, knowing well how happy they would be.

THE LAKE ISLE OF INISFREE
By William Butler Yeats 1865-1939

I will arise and go now, and go to Inisfree,
And a small cabin build there, of
Clay and wattles made,
Nine bean rows will I have there,
A hive for the honey bee,
And live alone in the bee-loud glade.

And I shall have some peace there,
For peace comes dropping slow,
Dropping from the veils of the
Morning to where the cricket sings.
There midnight's all a glimmer, and
Noon a purple glow,
And evening full of the linnet's wings.

I will arise and go now, for always
Night and day,
I hear lake water lapping with low
Sounds by the shore,
While I stand on the roadway, or on
The pavements grey,
I hear it in the deep heart's core.

(Nobel Prizewinner for Literature, 1923).